FOSSIL COVE PRESS

GIANT MONSTERS SING SAD SONGS

A Short Story Collection

by

D. G. Valdron

GIANT MONSTERS SING SAD SONGS
FOSSIL COVE PRESS
1301 - 90 Garry Street, Wpg, Man, Canada, R3C 4J4

Copyright © 2019 by Denis George Arthur Valdron. The right of Denis George Arthur Valdron (D.G. Valdron) to be identified as the author of this work is asserted. All rights reserved. This Book is a work of review, commentary, and criticism. Reviews and commentaries are the opinions of the author.

Cover: Eldon Ardiente, artist

Fossils *previously published in Daikaiju Anthology, 2005, Agog! Press, Ed. Robert Hood and Robin Pen*
Tell Me *previously published in After Hours magazine Autum, 1994, Ed. William G. Raley*

Quotations from the Necronomicon taken from:
The Festival, H.P. Lovecraft, 1923 (public domain)
Through the Gates of the Silver Key, H.P. Lovecraft and E. Hoffman Price, 1923-1933, (public domain)
Call of Cthulhu H.P.Lovecraft, 1926 (public domain)
Life of Alhazred, personal correspondence, H.P.Lovecraft, personal correspondence, 1927 (public domain)
The Dunwich Horror, H.P. Lovecraft, 1928 (public domain)
The Return of the Sorcerer,' Clark Ashton Smith, 1931 (public domain)
The Plain of Sound, Ramsay Campbell, 1965 (© Ramsay Campbell acknowledged)

Issued in electronic and print formats
ISBN: 978-0-9879061-9-9 (ebook)
ISBN: 978-1-990860-98-0 (IngramSpark print/trade papberback)

No part of this book may be used or reproduced in form or by any means, including electronic or mechanical, or by any information storage and retrieval system, any manner whatsoever without the prior written permission of the publisher, except in the case of brief quotations embedded in reviews.

Text set in Garamond

GIANT MONSTERS SING SAD SONGS

Table of Contents

Introduction Melancholy Nightmares

I'm not sure about this whole notion of introductions and afterwards, talking about your work. It seems to me, that these stories should stand or fall on their own. But it seems to be the thing to do. So here goes…

Horror is often an optimistic genre. Not that Dracula killing off your family, or Gamera trashing your city is really optimistic when you think about it. But the arc of horror stories is usually about evil or chaos showing up uninvited, corruption seeping in, the bad guys making their move, and ultimately, it's about triumph. The behemoth is sent to the bottom of the ocean, the werewolf gets a silver bullet, the masked killer is defeated, and the good guy/girl triumphs.

Most horror is ultimately about victory, it's about overcoming evil. Good horror is when evil gives us a run for its money. But ultimately, it goes down.

Except… What about the monsters that never intended to be monsters? The mad scientists who were just people who strayed from the path?

What about the people killed along the way? What about the scars that won't ever heal? What about the cost of that battle between good and evil? The ones who got crushed along the way? The lives lost, good and bad, the suffering, the grief?

Buried in the triumphant stories of good ultimately defeating evil, I think that there's a thread of melancholy.

There's sadness and loss in our stories of monsters.

Thanks

Fossils

G– stopped outside my penthouse the other morning, as I lay in bed. His weathered face, profiled outside the picture window, startled me. He seemed quite close enough to touch.

I moved carefully, many thoughts running through my mind. I sat up slowly in bed and reached for the camera I had fortuitously left by my nightstand.

Was the picture window one way glass? I didn't know, but it didn't seem likely. Could G– see through it? Could G–'s eye make out a human shape through it? Perhaps G–, like a dog or some other predator, focused best on movement?

With G– and the others like him, there are only questions and an occasional lethal answer.

Still, I reached for the camera. G– stood there immobile like a statue. With shaking hands I fitted the zoom lens, adjusted the focus and snapped off image after image, saving them to the chip. The click of the shutter and whine of the electrics were unbearably loud to me. At one point, I thought I saw G–'s ear twitch, but it was just his weight shifting.

I ran out of image slots. I sat in bed waiting for that baleful profile to turn towards me. But it didn't.

After five minutes G– took another step and passed from view.

I laid back in bed, uttering a prayer to gods I no longer believed in.

I do not believe in gods, but if they are, they do not require my belief to exist.

G– exists, he does not require our belief.

&&&

When I was a little boy in school, they taught us about dinosaurs and fossils.

Fossils were made when, ever so slowly, little bits of mineral took the place of organic material like bone or wood. Eventually, the whole thing was nothing but mineral, stone taking the place of what had once been alive.

Sometimes there was no living matter to replace, just an impression left behind like a footprint and filled in by time. All dinosaurs, we were told, are known only by fossils.

I remember the little girl in the desk in front of mine put up her hand and asked the question.

"What about G–?"

&&&

While waiting for the image slots to save into the art drive, I loaded the camera with a new chip and finished inspecting my lenses.

After a quick breakfast of canned shrimp, I headed down the stairs to the main floor. I contemplated taking the elevator, but G– was in the neighborhood, and the noise of machinery might attract his attention.

Probably not, but you never know.

The Kaiju were reported to be extremely sensitive, though to what, no one was quite sure. Magnetic fields, electrical current, sound waves, light and darkness. Who could know for sure?

G– was out of sight by the time I'd reached the main floor and walked out into the street. I walked up to one of his footprints.

It was fourteen meters long by seven wide, and approximately two meters deep in the center. The edges were barely crumbling, the detail was superb.

Briefly I considered taking a picture of it. But I already had more than enough pictures of G–'s footprints and there was no additional context that would lend the image interest or perspective.

I looked down the street. G– had been walking west. Three strides from the penthouse had taken G– to the end of the street where he turned left. I felt another seismic tremor as G–, beyond my line of sight, took his next step.

Giant Monsters Sing Sad Songs / Page 2

I'd had enough of G– for the day; I turned and began walking east.

It was a fine new day in deserted Tokyo.

&&&

I spent the rest of the day breaking into apartments. In one, I stayed to watch a television documentary on a battery powered set. It was about the refugee camps. I found myself wondering if any of the people I saw in the documentary were the ones who had lived in this apartment.

I went shopping in the Kyoru family grocery. The produce was off, but the dry goods and canned fruit were abundant. From there, I took my selections to the Konishawa-Saru restaurant. It was a little dusty, and the kitchen was disordered, but I managed well enough.

The Konishawa had been a four star restaurant, but I wouldn't give it better than three stars tonight. The regular chef must be off, I decided.

&&&

Man is an arrogant beast, I think sometime. We are like ants building our nests by the seashore, thinking we have mastered eternity. Then the next wave comes and takes it all away.

We forget how small we are next to the world. Foolishly, we imagine that the fact of our existence is proof of our divinity.

We thought we were the masters of the Earth.

In 1956 we discovered that we were wrong.

In 1956 G– came, the first of the Kaiju.

&&&

The next day, I stumbled across a group of people in the boulevard of Cherry Blossoms. I was startled; sometimes I would go for days without seeing anyone.

They were all gathered around an object near the center of the boulevard.

Down the center, of course, G–'s tail had dragged, crushing legions of trees to matchsticks.

Diffidently, I walked up to them. I find I am unused to company, these days.

One of them looked up and called to me. I knew him, Ryushi, the physicist.

"Kenjiro," Ryushi called, "come and take a photograph of what we have found."

The object was leaf shaped, two meters long, one and a half across, smooth and glossy black. It was convex, with a sharply curving hook at one end. I took four pictures from different angles. One shot had Ryushi in it to show scale.

One of the others, Manage, had found a length of pipe and began levering it over. While he did this, I punched in a subtext to accompany the images I had taken.

"Is it hot," Gemma asked. Gemma was one of our resident mad poets.

"Only mildly radioactive," Akira said, "equivalent to a few months normal exposure. Also, slightly above ambient temperature."

I lifted an eyebrow, but did not look up. He must have touched it then, to know the warmth.

That was enough for me. I joined Manage at his labors, grunting as we flipped it over. The concave side was gray with layers of ridges, as if it had partially melted. I ran my hand over its surface.

"It's a scale," said the woman, unnecessarily. I looked up at her.

"It's a piece of G–."

&&&

Her name was Sumiko. I discovered this as we sat on a bench and watched the army helicopter cart away the scale.

She was new to deserted Tokyo, just arrived. She was a philosopher and she has been diagnosed with cancer.

A philosopher here to study G–? I should be shocked, but I find nothing surprises me anymore. Perhaps more than scientists, it is philosophers who are needed to grapple with the existence of G– and his kind.

Politely, I told her the name of my mortality. I tell her of yesterday's encounter with G– and invite her to my penthouse to look at my stills.

Graciously, she accepts my invitations.

In the distance, we hear G–'s lonely roar.

&&&

There are probably less than a thousand people living in deserted Tokyo. Counting everyone. Counting mad poets, artists, photographers, journalists, eccentrics and scientists of every stripe, soldiers, police, thieves, looters, opportunists as well as simple fools and madmen. Although perhaps we are all fools and madmen to be here.

And of course, there is G–.

G– is in Tokyo. But does G– live? Perhaps that depends on what you define as life. I read a biology text once which set out seven basic criteria to determine whether something is truly alive.

I am not sure that G– fulfills all the requirements.

But in morose moments, I am not sure that I do, either.

The test of life is whether it can reproduce itself.

&&&

"This is a sumptuous home," Sumiko says, as I prepare supper in the penthouse. We took the elevator up. G– is far from us. "You must be a very wealthy man."

I cough, discretely wiping droplets of blood from my lips with a handkerchief. I let the stained cloth drop into a waste basket.

"The comforts of a city are at our fingertips," I tell her, "the least we can do is enjoy it."

She seems mildly shocked by my veiled admission of breaking and entering.

In the movies, looters are shot on sight. In deserted Tokyo, there is nothing petty thievery and vandalism can accomplish that approaches G–'s awful potential.

Out in the refugee camps, Tokyo, the real Tokyo of people continues as best it can. Men in cloth tents buy and sell fortunes and children play in the grass outside.

Perhaps I should suggest this to Gemma. He could make a poem from it.

"Would you sleep in the Emperor's bed?" she asks.

It seems the authorities have allocated to her a modest apartment, and like a good Japanese, she has not thought to question it.

Why? In an empty city, I could sleep in a different penthouse every night.

"Only if you were to join me," I tell her.

She blushes and drops her eyes.

I am touched.

At dinner, of course, I am a perfect gentleman. Our conversation is animated and polite. Although he is always in our minds, we never mention G–.

&&&

I chose this penthouse because of the magnificent view of the harbor. You can see all the way from the docks and shipyards in the south, to the houseboats, now largely absent, and waterfront palaces ringing the north.

On the east side of the penthouse we watch G– in the harbor far away. He stands in the water, like some savagely thrown outcrop of rough volcanic rock. A storm caught in a moment of time, rendered in stone. Not a bad description of G–.

He has not moved in two hours.

Once he did not move for four days. I recorded it with time lapse photography and a battery of four cameras on tripods, tied into the household power source and downloading directly into a dedicated art-drive.

Later, I watched the accelerated record, clouds flicking past, day turning to night in minutes. G– stood there like a god, impervious to time.

Perhaps G– is a god. I will have to remind myself to ask Sumiko for her views on this.

The light is poor for photography tonight, and in any event, I have many, many, many images of G– at the harbor. I do not use my camera. Normally, at this hour, I retire to the bedroom and tend to my lenses.

But tonight, I have a guest.

Sumiko does not tire of watching G–. I am happy to pass the time in idle conversation.

Giant Monsters Sing Sad Songs / Page 6

"Each of the Kaiju are different," I say. "G— is obviously derived from a dinosaur, but which one?"

Not all dinosaurs, it seems, are known from fossils. Or perhaps there are simply different sorts of fossils.

"A tyrannosaur?" Sumiko replies, startling me for a second.

"A common fallacy," I reply, "actually, the Taiwan Kaiju is thought to be a tyrannosaurid, but most learned opinion places G—'s origins in the Jurassic rather the Cretaceous periods."

"She's so huge," Sumiko whispers, "she seems to glow."

I notice that she refers to G— as female. It is a matter of preference, I suppose. Irrelevant in the end. G— transcends all things.

In fact, G— does glow, softly so you can only see it on moonless nights. All of the Kaiju, radioactive monsters that they are, glow.

G— begins to move suddenly, lumbering among the docks. We hear a distant crashing as G— pulls a wharf down.

"What is she doing?" Sumiko asks.

"G— is building a nest."

&&&

G— first surfaced in 1956, striding onto Japan and burning his way through Tokyo. The pleasant wide boulevards of modern Tokyo are the legacies of G—'s wholesale destruction. And of the Americans.

We battled fiercely, side by side with the Americans, until G— returned to the cold waters.

We thought we'd won.

But G— returned a few years later. Then, one by one, the rest of the Kaiju appeared up and down the Asian coast, with a few stragglers in North America and Europe.

G— has been sighted fourteen times since then. We learned that the Kaiju could not be destroyed. So, when G— after fourteen years of relatively peaceful behavior, surfaced and began to head for Tokyo, the city was evacuated.

&&&

G–'s image fills the wall I use for a projection screen. I enhance and magnify, zooming in on the teeth. After moments of blurriness, they come into focus, split screen close ups of upper and lower dentition.

The teeth are a dirty white, built up in jagged layers like concrete inexpertly sculpted. Spikes radiate outwards from the edges. But upper and lower teeth curve in what we recognize as the classic carnivore's dentition. The upper teeth are smaller, with rounded tips and longer spikes radiating from the borders.

I check my readouts; the average size of the seven teeth in the frame is three meters.

"It's so strange," Sumiko says, "I guess I expected them to be smooth."

"Perhaps they were, originally," I say. "But awesome processes have been at work to create a being so vast. My guess is that they are smooth inside the mouth. Those spikes facing outward along the edges are probably melt from the creature's breath."

"The plasma breath," she says.

"Not plasma," I correct, "steam, superheated to 10,000 degrees and ejected at something like five thousand pounds per square inch. Sufficient to cut a battleship in half."

&&&

In 1968 the U.S. fourth fleet, led by the battleship New Jersey and the aircraft carrier Montana, encountered G– off the Kuril Islands.

In a pitched battle lasting less than a day, G– sliced apart the carrier, punched holes in the battleship, and sent three quarters of the fleet to the bottom of the sea, taking no significant damage himself.

A hydrogen bomb was dispatched, but by the time the bomber arrived, G– was deep beneath the ocean.

I was ten years old when it happened, a little boy from Fukien province, and I remembered cheering to hear of the Americans humbled.

&&&

"Tell me about your book," I ask her over lunch. Days have passed and she is a frequent visitor now. For that reason, I seldom go out in the mornings, instead preparing for her mid-day visit.

I was surprised to learn that she wrote a book. I thought I'd read all the books on the Kaiju. I was surprised that I'd missed hers.

"It was only a thesis," she says modestly, "published with limited circulation."

I wait politely, sipping my tea.

"It dealt with how human societies construct the concept of the Kaiju."

"You think perhaps they are fictional?" I ask, just politely enough not to be mocking.

We both glance the bowl on the table between us, at the seismic ripples of G—'s latest footfall. Generally, he takes five to ten minutes between one step and the next, although he can move much faster. Much, much faster.

"The phenomena of the Kaiju," she says carefully, "are real enough, as is the phenomena of storm and waves. But we must ask what society makes of these phenomena. Once storms were thought to be living things, embodiments of the will of the gods."

There is an odd precision to these words. I wonder if she is quoting her thesis.

"Now we have the Kaiju. Are they the will of the gods? Science gone wrong? Simple animals? Are they even alive, or is that simply something we need to believe of them? What something is or does, and what we think it is, those may be different things."

"I find," I say softly, "that the fact of G— overwhelms anything I might say or think of him."

Still, her words echo thoughts of my own.

&&&

The first Kaiju I ever saw was A— on Okinawa Island. This was in 1975 when it had become known as the peaceful Kaiju.

A normally slow moving quadruped, just a couple of hundred meters long, it had surfaced in 1964. After it's now famous confrontations with G– in 1965 and M– in 1966 it had settled down to a sedentary peaceful existence, devouring groves in isolated areas.

There was, of course, no evidence that it needed the trees for sustenance. That seemed to have been archaic biological programming at work. The needs of the Kaiju are obscure. They do not seem to breathe or eat as we do. G– seems as comfortable, miles underwater, as he is in downtown Tokyo on dry land.

In any case, A– was remarkably placid for a Kaiju, taking no notice of the approach of humans.

As must be inevitable, a clandestine tourist trade arose. I, with a group of wild young friends, went to see the monster.

I remember that we had been drinking on the way and making many a joke. I was flirting then, with a young woman I would, ultimately, never sleep with.

Everything changed when it came into view.

How to describe the mind warping immensity of it? We all fell silent. It was like we had come to some titanic European renaissance cathedral. A living cathedral.

Even then, I knew that while A– was a respectable sized Kaiju, it was far from the greatest. It was less than a quarter of the mass of G–, for example.

For an hour we watched it. Then, recovering some of my boldness from the journey, I walked right up to it, and leaned nonchalantly against a leg that could have crushed a small house. Being there, touching it, was a bizarre sensation that lasted a moment, until the creature decided to move. Then I ran like a rabbit.

In my files there is a picture of me leaning against it. I have a cocky insouciant grin. It is not a good picture of A– however. Since then, I have taken many better pictures of the Kaiju, and particularly of G–.

The guide was beside himself at my actions, of course. It was radioactive, and forbidden to approach so close.

The moment changed my life, from then on the Kaiju would be my obsession. The relationship foundered, especially after it was found that I was sterile. I have often wondered if that was the result of the encounter, or if I was always this way.

Perhaps, this, ultimately, was where my leukemia came from.

&&&

I encountered Ryushi on my walk today.

I was not pleased.

I find that, except for Sumiko, I have little use for human company.

I ignored him, but he insisted on following me around and chattering like a monkey.

"Have you heard from Geological Survey?" He asks. "They found a post-nuclear site in the Gobi desert?"

I shrugged.

"It dates to the Jurassic. This might have been the birthplace of G–, possibly some of the others."

Finally, I stop.

"I do not care where they come from," I tell him.

Behind his thick glasses, his little boy face looks shocked.

"It does not matter whether G– was born in a lake of fire, or found under a cabbage leaf, Ryushi. G– is here now."

"But…"

"Haven't you ever experienced it, Ryushi?" I ask him. "Or have you merely measured. Such a creature mocks our pretensions. It does not care about your measurements. It does not care what we think. There is no past. There is no future. There is only the now, and in the now, there is only G–."

These are more words than I have ever spoken to Ryushi. Embarrassed at my anger and at my passion, I walk away quickly. Ryushi stays behind.

Later, I find G– exquisitely framed between two tall buildings. He is once again motionless and torpid. Breaking into the first, I climb, taking several shots of G– from the windows of each floor. I fill chip after chip.

However, as I am climbing down, intending to capture him from the angles of the opposite building, G— rouses again and walks ponderously away. His tail brushes the building I am in. The structure rocks and the front part collapses away like a veil of sand. It is several hours before I can safely find my way out.

It is night when I finally arrive home. I collapse on the bed, exhausted, not even downloading my chips. They can wait until tomorrow.

&&&

"Where does G— come from?" Sumiko asks as these latest pictures of G— are displayed on the wall. This used to be a banquet room, but I find it serves well as a projection area. I line the walls and ceiling with projected images.

Sumiko lays on her belly, naked on the futon. I lay beside her, with my arm thrown possessively across her shoulders. In my hand, the control triggers and manipulates the sequence of images.

We have consummated our relationship. It was messy and wet and not at all safe. But then, in deserted Tokyo, what have we to fear?

Certainly not a virus.

As we made love, as I was insider her, I remember wondering if our cancers touched as well. Perhaps on some level beneath passionate flesh, rogue tissue, cells in riot, made contact, kissed, embraced, exchanged information.

But there will be no issue. Not from us, nor from our cancers.

I consider her question.

"It is hard to say in G—'s case. Clearly, he is derived from dinosaurs. Some of the Kaiju are easy. A— for example, is an ankylosaurid. O— in Taiwan is obviously a tyronnosaurian. But G—?"

"A stegosaur?" she offers.

"The back plates? The relatively small head on a long neck? The small forelimbs compared to the hind?" I offer. "That's one theory."

"But remember those teeth I showed you," I remind her. "Carnivore teeth. I tend to think he's something off the allosaur line, possibly something not yet discovered."

"And the spiny plates on the back?" She asks.

I shrug.

"Obviously part of G–'s cooling system. Possibly it's a Kaiju growth, or maybe a mutation in the original creature. Perhaps a species of allosaurians developed stegosaur plates independently, and we haven't found them yet. It has been known to happen."

There are strange things beneath the Earth. Sometimes they rise up.

&&&

The thirty six known Kaiju constitute taxonomist nightmare. Most are clearly reptiles, relatively identifiable offshoots of archosaur lines such as dinosaurs. Their origins are placed between eighty and two hundred million years ago. A few, however, are mammals of substantially more recent vintage. One is a bird of unknown provenance. One is a vastly mutated coelacanth. Another is a five tentacled octopus. Four are arguably, impossibly, insects or arthropods. Three cannot be classified.

&&&

"When the Kaiju first came..." Sumiko is reading from her book.

We are sitting on the east side of the penthouse, watching G– slowly make its way to the waters.

"...we identified them with the atom bomb. Because they were radioactive and wrought great destruction, we believed that they were the spawn of the Americans atomic testing. Mutated animals, but more than that, we saw them as symbols of foreign recklessness and destruction."

"Many in the scientific community accepted this thesis, in spite of the obviously ancient traits of several.

"Only the Americans, with their lingering guilt over Hiroshima and Nagasaki, and their commitment to nuclear arsenals rejected this view.

"The Americans had tamed the atom. In doing so, they believed they had controlled the fundamental forces of nature. To the Americans, the Kaiju were simply a form of nature, of animal. Ultimately, they were merely an engineering problem to be assessed and solved."

That, I thought, rolling the words around in my head, was probably before the fourth fleet.

&&&

All of the Kaiju share certain traits. Their immense size: the smallest of them dwarf the largest blue whales. Colossal mass: often measured in thousands of tons.

Most are found somewhere along the Pacific ring of fire. The few exceptions appear to derive from other volcanic areas. In some undetermined way, plate tectonics seems to play a part in their cosmic biology.

The Kaiju are invariably highly radioactive and their defenses often incorporate this radioactivity. Their flesh does not appear to be composed of living matter as we understand it. They are best likened to walking nuclear reactors.

The Kaiju appear to be very territorial, often ranging widely to confront each other.

The Kaiju have often attacked human sites and installations. It is uncertain why. Some feel that it is a simple matter of humanity being so widespread that no matter where the Kaiju go, and they go where they will, they encounter us. Others argue that the sheer size of manmade sites and constructions invoke their territorial urges. Still others point to a wide range of emanations, sonic, electrical, magnetic, that might attract their attention.

Some simply say that they are the will of the gods.

Who can be sure?

&&&

Once, when I was much less a hermit, only new come to deserted Tokyo, the mad poet Gemma confided his theory to me.

"Seismics," he said, drawing the word out over an exhalation of marijuana. He passed the cigarette to me and I puffed politely, looking at him with curiosity.

"It was the nuclear tests that woke the monsters," he explained. "But not the radiation, not even the electromagnetic pulse, as everyone thinks. It was the seismics."

He grinned.

"The seismic waves of the nuclear blasts mimicked those of a cometary bombardment."

He blew smoke rings.

"Tell me, Kenjiro, have you ever heard of cyclic extinction, of the slate wiped clean every seventeen million years. They blame cometary or meteor bombardment, but let's be reasonable, that wouldn't wipe out everything all over the world."

"It's the Kaiju. Every seventeen million years the comets come to wake the Kaiju, who sterilize the world for the next cycle of life.

"We've woken them early, that's why they are confused. Now we wait to see if they'll go back to sleep or wake fully."

"What if they wake fully?" I asked.

Manage simply sucked a lung full of smoke from his cigarette and let it out, laughing crazily.

&&&

"Where does G— come from?" Sumiko asks.

It seems to me that she has asked this question before.

We are in bed again. Our cancers have engaged in sweaty intercourse, carrying their human parts along.

I look at the ceiling.

"I will tell you the theory. Have you ever heard of post-nuclear sites?" I ask.

"Atom bomb craters?"

"No. The first one was discovered in Africa, almost thirty years ago. It was a kind of natural atomic pile. Several others have been identified, all dead for millions of years, of course."

She levers herself up on one arm to look at me. I admire the slight sway of her small breasts.

"How can that be?"

I am surprised at how little she knows of material things. The choice of the philosopher, I suppose.

Giant Monsters Sing Sad Songs / Page 15

"Radioactive materials are always decaying. In the future, there will be less. That means, in the past, there was more. The million years ago, there were twice as many radioactives in the Earth as there are now. Ten million years before that, twice as many as then, and so on.

"In some places, these radioactive materials were washed down streams. They accumulated and concentrated in ponds and lakes. Most times, this came to nothing.

"But sometimes these concentrations built, fission actually began to take place. Nuclear reactions began, accelerating the decay of some elements, creating new ones. Fed by streams, moderated by rainfalls and dehydration, the processes were remarkably like those in modern nuclear plants."

"This is very interesting," she tells me, "but what does it have to do with the Kaiju, with G–?"

"Animals drink in those ponds and streams. They are poisoned by radiation. Many die."

"Some probably die in the water. Their bodies occasionally floating down to the bottom of the nuclear ponds.

"What a strange environment it must be. There are no bacteria to speed the normal processes of decomposition.

"Instead, the tissues are saturated in radioactive soup. The long shattered strands of DNA are joined by ions of lead and graphite, uranium or silicon. Our bodies, our cells are merely chemical factories. Who is to say that an effective chemical factory might not be converted to a nuclear one?

"Slowly the dead beast wakes to a new kind of existence. Its body accreting new elements, new internal fires light. A self-perpetuating, feedback based system refines and expands through pathways already made, it perfects itself, growing slowly but without limit."

"Kenjiro," she whispers, "do you think it is true?"

I laugh. I have seen G–.

"It doesn't matter," I tell her.

&&&

The next time I see Sumiko, she is pale and shaking. I almost expect her hair to turn white. I take her home from where I find her. Her teeth chatter, she is not aware of my touch. I bathe her and dry her and sit with her until she speaks.

Her story is not, at first, coherent.

She had been out on the Emperor's way, towards the Ministry of Finance. G– passed by.

That was all.

G– had been moving quickly, barely pausing between steps. Sumiko had stopped and looked up, and there, through the branches of leafless trees, she had seen G– looming above her. She had looked up a hundred and fifty meters of scaled not flesh, a titanic construction of not-bone and not-sinew, as it gracefully passed her.

It took seven steps to the Ministry of Finance, vaporized several structures with an incandescent roar, and proceeded through the burning wreckage without once hesitating.

It takes her two hours to relate this.

I feel a kind of cruel and burning satisfaction.

This is G–, not some footprint, not a scale by the roadside, or a picture or a figure softened by miles of distance. Not some abstract metaphor explored in dry academia.

She has seen G–, finally. Seen the truth of G–. A vastness that drives out all thought, all knowledge, all comprehension.

Eventually she goes to sleep.

I step out onto the west deck of the penthouse. I feel G–'s footfalls in the night, less than five minutes apart. G– roars once.

He's restless tonight.

&&&

I had a dream once.

G– and the other Kaiju walked the Earth under a vast red sun. It was a barren world, without gust of wind, without oceans, without life. Even the moon was but a ring of dust. The Kaiju walked, the last things on Earth, eternal and unchanging. Listening to things only they could hear. Following things only they could see.

&&&

Giant Monsters Sing Sad Songs / Page 17

"The failure in Vietnam..." Again, Sumiko reads from her manuscript. "And the destruction of the fourth fleet, were just two of the factors contributing to the collapse of American optimism in the seventies. Perhaps equally significant was the first of a series of bracing recessions and the slow economic decline and eclipse by other nations."

I must be honest and say that I find much of it abstruse and tedious. It is of interest only to other philosophers, and perhaps not many of them. But her early sections show traces of flash and insight. I make it read her to me, hoping it will help her regain herself.

She will never completely recover from the sight of G–, of course. None of us will.

She belongs here now, in deserted Tokyo, with the lost and the mad.

"The seventies marked the end of the various constructions and devices to control or defend against the Kaiju. Barriers, electric walls, laser shields, some of these had experienced limited success. But all had proven ineffective against one or another of the Kaiju. Their appearance seemed to goad the creatures."

"Nor could the great beasts be killed. It had become apparent that nothing short of a nuclear explosion might be sufficient to destroy one of them. More, it was become equally apparent that killing a Kaiju would merely liberate its atomic reactions from internal regulation. It posed more problems than the creature itself.

"Instead, unable to resolve the problem of the Kaiju as animals, the perception changed. From spawn of the atom, to wild beasts, they came to be perceived as simply a force of nature. The Kaiju were like hurricanes and earthquakes, powerful, unstoppable, irrational but ultimately, transient.

"As the eighties developed, the strategy became increasingly one of avoidance. When a Kaiju approached, the town or city was simply evacuated. When the Kaiju departed, as they invariably did, the population returned or reconstructed elsewhere.

"Interestingly, this strategy of dealing with Kaiju such as G–," I watch her involuntary shiver, "appears to be strongly predicated on the perception of the Kaiju as, in their ultimate form, inanimate. A perception, oddly enough, not supported by initial evaluations, but rather, one forced upon us through our inability to properly intellectualize the phenomena..."

Sumiko begins to cry. Closing the book, her face contorts, tears streaming down her cheeks. Great racking sobs tear out of her. I hold her until it passes.

I wish I felt more.

&&&

That night, I wake to find her sitting cross legged in bed, staring at me. Our eyes lock.

"I don't want to be like you," she says finally. Her voice is soft and full of regret.

"It is too late," I tell her.

I roll over and go to sleep.

In the morning, when I wake, she is gone.

I busy myself, caring for my lenses, organizing my art drives. She does not appear for lunch. Finally, I go out to look for G–.

&&&

G– has wandered out into the suburbs. It is time for the assault on the nest. It has been in the planning, off and on, for months. We are all called in.

I go with Sumiko. She says little now. A coldness has entered our relationship. I suspect that we never will sleep in the Emperor's bed together.

"Do you know what Manage calls you," she said to me the other day.

"Man of stone," she said.

Ryushi is there, eyes too large behind bottle-thick glasses. He flashes his myopic grin as he hands out radiation suits.

I know what Ryushi is all about. He is like the blind men in the story of the elephant. He has persuaded himself that blindness, the restriction of his vision, will help him see more clearly. The truth is merely that he does not see at all.

Are we so different?

Giant Monsters Sing Sad Songs / Page 19

Radiation suits are a needless precaution for such as we. But I put mine on anyway, to please Ryushi. It is not every day that you venture into the dragon's lair.

Farther on there are men I do not know. They are dispensing rock climbing gear. They seem experienced.

We are broken into teams, climbing the mounds that G— has thrown up around its nest. It is not a difficult climb, even though the slopes are steep and the debris is often unstable.

But it is disturbing. We grapple upon the crushed and melted remains of buildings and automobiles, past artifacts as small as a doll's hand, or as out of place as a computer keyboard. All of it mixed willy nilly with total indifference to any human scheme.

There is nothing living here, not seagulls or rats or weeds. Nothing can live here.

I am almost afraid of what we will find on the other side.

As it turns out, the other side is just more of the same. It is as if someone has taken all the artifacts of human civilization, stirred them in some great cauldron, and used them to build a Martian landscape. It is a strange and inhuman world we walk through. It dwarfs us with G—'s unseen presence.

The Geiger counter is going wild.

In several places there are deep pools of unknown liquid glowing in many colors. Samples are taken. From the corners of our eye we see furtive movements. G—'s parasites, creatures like fleas or ticks, but half the size of a man. These things live freely here.

This is not a place for human beings.

Finally, in the center, we come to the ovoids. They are covered loosely with debris.

"Possibly droppings," Ryushi says.

"Eggs," Sumiko says.

"Impossible," I say. Life reproduces, that is what life is. That which reproduces. The Kaiju are not alive.

"Eggs," Sumiko says.

"No," I say, "they must be sterile, like hens eggs. Products of an ancient biology gone wrong."

Giant Monsters Sing Sad Songs / Page 20

"Eggs," Sumiko says.

The others are shaken, I can see that.

They are trying to absorb this new development.

&&&

"I am leaving," Sumiko tells me as we have one of our now infrequent lunches.

"Why?" I ask bluntly, fearing the reply.

"They've found a new Kaiju, buried on the Kamchatka peninsula. I've joined the expeditionary force."

I absorb this news quietly.

"Seismic survey's discovered it. We think it is dead. There is much to discover."

Impossible, I think, a Kaiju cannot die. It is forever.

Kaiju cannot reproduce, the thought lashes me.

I find I have little to say, as she leaves. It is not as if I need her, or anyone else. She is right. I am a man of stone.

How did I get this way?

What did the Kaiju do to me?

&&&

I have another dream.

I dream of G— in her nest in the ruins of deserted Tokyo, brooding eternally, relentlessly over glowing eggs which may never hatch. Perhaps this is truly G—, a being torn from the belly of time, holding a moment preserved.

Perhaps this is what a god is.

I dream of the Americans, ant-like and confused, stirred by the knowledge of the eggs. They are flying through the air. They bring their own god, another instant torn from the belly of time. A scream of birth/death/love/hate/marriage....

Its name is H—.

The End

Flirtin' Out Back With the Sasquatch Kid

"The World's Only Authentic Bigfoot Museum" Dad read aloud as they drove down the highway.

Wendy looked up irritably from her tattered copy of Jane Eyre. The car was too hot and cramped, especially the back seat, which she had to share with a hyperactive weasel of a kid brother, Iggy.

"You aren't going to stop, dear?" Mom said. "We're already behind, I want to get to George and Grace before night."

"Stop!" howled Iggy. "Stop, stop, stop, stop!" He began kicking the back of the front seat.

"It's a holiday, Darling," Dad answered back to Mom. Somehow, they'd gotten very good at ignoring Iggy. Wendy couldn't imagine how.

"Besides," Dad said, "I bet the kids could use a chance to stretch their legs. Burn off some of that excess energy. Right, Champ?"

He directed that last to Iggy, Wendy knew.

They passed another sign, this one fifteen foot tall plywood cut-out of a grinning hairy ape, with a smaller grinning man perched on its shoulder. They were both waving. The sign underneath said, "Sasquatch Kid Museum, one mile."

Maybe the signs were like Burma Shave, Wendy thought. One every few hundred yards until you were there. She went back to her book.

"I wanna see the bigfoot!" Iggy howled, his nine year old's voice grated like broken glass. "I wanna see the monster."

"God," Wendy sniffed, "you're such a creep."

Iggy kicked her, so she kicked him back, which led to a flurry of kicks and slaps.

"Do I have to stop the car?" Dad asked, his voice harsh with warning.

"He started it," Wendy complained.

"We heard what you said," Dad told her, "you shouldn't provoke him."

"He provokes me all the time," Wendy complained, overwhelmed by the pungent unfairness of it all.

"Iggy's only nine, Wendy," Dad told her, "you're fourteen."

"Yeah," said Iggy, "you're fourteen."

He stuck his tongue out at her.

"Fine," Wendy said, putting as much frost in her voice as she could muster. She slammed the Jane Eyre shut and folded her arms across her chest.

"Let's go see the monster," Iggy said, he cautiously kicked the front seat once or twice for good measure.

"In a bit, Champ," his father told him.

Wendy's cheeks burned at this obvious favouritism. She tried to drill her eyes through the back of her parent's heads. But they paid no attention.

Why was the world always so damned unfair? She thought bitterly. Iggy got to run around like a wild animal, and nobody paid the least attention. If she did the least little thing they were down on her case. Nobody, not even Mom understood her. They didn't understand the powerful waves of feelings that would sweep over and leave her on the verge of weeping. She didn't belong in this family.

Wendy felt things. She felt things so much more vividly and intensely than her bug-like brother or her dull parents. Her real family, she thought suddenly, was Jane Eyre. Jane Eyre and Wuthering Heights and Sylvia Plath. It was books and poetry and the tortured intense souls who created it. Not the leaden plodders she was raised with.

Iggy was crowding her again, just the way he'd done a thousand times before on this road trip to their Uncle. She'd told him a thousand times to stop, and he hadn't listened and

Mom and Dad hadn't paid attention. Not the least bit of attention.

Mom and Dad were talking now, and not even paying attention.

Fine, she decided, she would just sit here. Life was so unfair.

They turned down a dirt road.

"That's one of the benefits of travelling by road," Dad was saying, "you can see all this neat stuff, like the Barb Wire Museum, or the World's Largest Ball of Twine or the Incredible Two Headed Snake..."

"The Hollywood Museum," Iggy chimed in.

That had been the absolute worst, she thought. The Hollywood Special Effects Museum, in some nowhere small town where she was sure nobody had ever so much as been to Hollywood. A couple of high school kids had filled their parents two car garage with papier mache dioramas with Ken and Barbie dolls dressed as Luke Skywalker and Princess Leia.

Iggy had loved it; they'd had to pry him out with a crowbar. Meanwhile, one of the pimple faced geeky teenagers had stared obsessively at her, all through the tour, as he'd told them about the movie his brother and he were going to make, and hinting about screen tests. Oh right, screen tests.

"These places have so much character," Dad was saying. "Not like big city places which are so bland and corporate. When you're looking at the two headed snake, you know its meaningless crap. But its meaningless crap that someone loves...that counts for something."

As far as Wendy was concerned, meaningless crap was meaningless crap.

She must have been adopted, she decided once again.

She was continually overwhelmed by the intensity and meaningfulness of life, and there was Dad, stopping to take a picture of the giant armadillo shell.

"We're on a deadline," Mom said, "I don't know if we have time. Besides, the tourist season is over, they probably aren't open."

"I'm sure that we can spare an hour or so, if they're open," Dad said.

"Let's do it," Iggy was practically bouncing in the back seat.

"Vote?" Dad asked. "I'll go for it."

"I don't think so," Mom said.

"Both hands for!" Iggy said.

"What about you, Princess?" Dad asked.

Wendy thought about it. Wandering around some goofy small town freak show and looking at a cow skeleton wired upright didn't much appeal to her.

"It doesn't matter," she said sullenly.

"We'll check it out then," Dad said.

The museum driveway was coming up, and he pulled onto it.

"Here we are," Dad said cheerily and unnecessarily. The pulled into the empty dirt parking lot. Ahead of them was an ungainly wooden frame construction, it looked like an old oversized farmhouse with a barn tacked onto the side. What looked like a large crude statue, a giant block of wood carved by chain saw, stood in front.

"THE SASQUATCH KID MUSEUM" a brightly coloured sign blared, and in smaller text, "Home of the World's Only Authentic Bigfoot: Peter Winston."

"I hope that they have a decent bathroom," Mom said, "for Wendy. It's that time."

"Mom," Wendy protested. She didn't like Mom referring to it like that in front of males. It was bad enough that she thought she could practically smell herself.

"Winston, Winston. Peter Winston..." Dad said softly. "I think I heard something about that a few years ago."

Wendy noticed that the parking lot was completely empty.

Iggy boiled out of the car. Mom and Dad, more leisurely, unbuckled their seat belt and stepped out.

Wendy sat and opened up Jane Eyre again.

Her door opened.

"Aren't you coming, sweety?" her mother asked.

"I'm fine," she said, "I'll just read."

"It's going to get awfully hot in the car," Mom said doubtfully.

I know how to suffer, Wendy thought to herself. "I'll be fine," she said.

"Wendy," her father had come around behind her mother, "it's a vacation, you can read any time. Now stop being such a pain in the ass and get out of the car."

There was just enough of an edge to his voice.

Wendy got out of the car.

"Fine," she said, choking on bitterness, "let's go see the Bigfoot. It's probably just some old gorilla suit."

"Leave the book in the car," Dad told her.

Her cheeks burned.

Dad locked the car doors behind them, as Wendy and her mother walked up the landing. Better safe than sorry, he always said, but the parking lot was painfully empty, Wendy noticed. Iggy was already there, practically dancing on the pedestal around the legs of the statue.

As they approached it, Wendy was struck by the amateurish crudeness of the heavyset apish figure; it looked like it had been carved by a caveman. Perhaps a caveman with a chain saw.

"It's ugly," she said.

Of course, Dad had to take pictures of it, and she and Iggy had to be in the pictures.

Behind the statue was the entrance. Above the doorway was writing. "What are men?" the doorway asked, "But apes trapped in unending childhood."

"Well," the father said, squinting doubtfully at the statue as they walked towards it, "it looks pretty interesting... I think this was in the news a few years back."

"There was a TV movie," the mother commented. "I think Marge taped it, but I never got around to watching it."

"It's famous," Iggy said, "come on. I want to see the Sasquatch Kid."

They walked through the door. There was an old man at the counter, watching television.

"Welcome," he said. He seemed friendly enough. "Here to see the Sasquatch Kid Museum?"

"No," said Iggy, "we want to see the Sasquatch Kid!"

Dad got that irritated look on his face for just a second.

"If it's open. We know it's late in the season," he told the man.

"That's all right," the man said, "the staff is off, but I can give you the tour myself."

He held out his hand.

"Ben Winston," he said, "father of the Sasquatch Kid, curator of this museum."

Dad shook hands solemnly and introduced the family. Wendy shook hands with the old man. His grip was dry and firm. Admission was five dollars a head. The old man bowed as he lowered the velvet rope and ushered them inside.

The first room was mainly just photographs on the wall. It showed the old man, much younger in the pictures. He was with a woman who was probably his wife.

There were baby pictures, "Peter Winston, at one month," the captions would say. "Peter Winston," a grinning toddler lying on a bear skin rug, "Six months."

"Most people don't get much out of this gallery," Ben told her folks, "but for me, this is my favourite place."

This was lamer than the Princess Leia Barbie dolls, she thought sourly. She couldn't believe they'd paid actual money to look at someone's baby pictures.

"We were farmers," the old man, Ben, was telling her Mom and Dad. "We'd been farming for four generations. It was hard work, but honest. We did all right."

She scanned through the photographs of the wall. Peter Winston, grade one. Peter Winston, at the state fair. Family pictures. Classroom shots, Peter Winston in his grade four class.

"We'd been married for four years when we had Peter. He was a beautiful baby. Perfectly normal. All through his childhood, he was right as rain, you couldn't say he was different. Looking back now, that's probably what makes it hardest. Back then, I think it made us slow to spot the changes."

In glass cases, there were baby clothes laid out neatly. Children's toys. Rattles, little cars. Coloring books. It was like her parents bronzing her baby shoes, but carried to ridiculous embarrassing extremes.

In the pictures she watched him taking his first step, grinning into the camera. There were kindergarten group photos. Another: Him standing proud and alone in his scout uniform. Another: Squirming on his mother's knee in a photomat booth.

More photographs. Peter as a gap toothed ten year old. At the fair with his family. Uniformed and sitting with his little league softball team.

Another: Peter with his father. The caption said he was twelve years old, but already he was taller than his father by a good two inches.

Peter Winston, age thirteen, a photograph announced. In the photograph, his dark eyes flashed, he'd had straight features, and thick, full wavy hair. He'd become, she thought to herself, a handsome youth.

By his thirteenth birthday, the caption continued, Peter had stood six feet seven inches tall.

He looked older, she thought, and then realized that he had gotten heavy. He no longer had the slenderness of youth, but rather, the solid thickness of a much older man. His face was still youthful.

"Wendy, Wendy," Iggy yelled, rushing back. He grabbed her hand and tugged, "Come see this room! It has dinosaurs and everything."

Iggy pulled her into a side room, cluttered with photographs and old fossils.

"Dinosaurs are birds," he explained, pointing. "But nobody could prove it because birds had a bone that dinosaurs didn't have. Clavicles. They'd lost it, but then they'd found it."

She had no idea what he was talking about, and found it hard to care. She sighed; he'd just go on without her.

Wendy read the explanation over the dinosaur/birds display. It was all about hidden genes and off switches. There had been an argument over whether birds had descended from dinosaurs. The crux of it had been that birds had a bone, a clavicle, that dinosaurs didn't, but dinosaurs' ancestors also had the bone. The idea was that dinosaurs couldn't have given rise to birds because they lacked that particular skeletal feature that birds possessed.

But dinosaurs had never really lost the missing bone; it was still in their genes. It had just been "switched off," made dormant somehow, so that the bone never actually developed. The upshot of the presentation was that when the birds had needed it, they'd switched it back on again.

There was a home-made model of a DNA molecule, probably some science fair project, and more stuff about genetic off switches. Another display compared drawings of a man and a chimpanzee and announced proudly that chimps and humans shared ninety-five per cent of their genetic code.

She stared at a picture of a baby chimp, erect carriage, high forehead. But for the fur, it looked almost like a person. Solemn and thoughtful.

"Alleles," Iggy popped the words out of nowhere.

Wendy jumped.

"What?" she said, irritated.

"Alleles," Iggy said, "they're pieces of genes. They do different things. Sometimes, when a particular sequence of genes is of no use, it's easier and faster in evolutionary terms to simply stick an allele as an off switch, to disregard that part of the sequence, than de-evolving the gene. Animals are full of gene sequences that are of no use, and have been turned off, so they're all still there even when they don't function."

"What are you gibbering about?" she snapped. Maybe he'd read it off one of the cards. Iggy had the disconcerting trick of talking with startling maturity about some arcane subject. As if, for a few minutes, he was actually channelling some grown up in a lab coat.

"We're just apes stuck in infant stages," he told her, "but all the full ape gene sequences are there. They just got turned off by alleles. What happened to the Sasquatch Kid was that the off switches didn't work. So all the gene sequences kicked in, and he kept on growing. It could happen to any of us."

There was an odd gleam in his eye as he said this. Ten years old and bright and at the bottom of everyone's pecking order. The idea of being ten feet tall and strong enough to overturn a Buick was compelling.

"I bet you'd like to be a big smelly ape," she spat out at him.

His eyes hardened. Snap! The ten year old hellion was back. "Well you're practically there already," he said, "the smelly part, anyway."

"You jerk..." she snapped.

But he was off into the side gallery; she followed him, flushed with irritation.

That section was on human freaks. Giants of all sorts. Dog faced boys. Hairy men and women. People with grotesquely swollen features. Wendy thought it was gross, but it fascinated Iggy.

She left him there.

She returned to the room she'd left and continued on into the next gallery.

There was a huge school picture where Peter, towered over his classmates and teachers. There were more pictures. Framed on the wall were faded clippings of newspaper articles about the "Caidinville Giant." Occasionally a phrase would stand out...local prodigy...potential football superstar...no end in sight.

At fourteen, Peter was over seven feet tall. The easy grins and laughter of the childhood photographs was gone. Peter looked haunted, worried, and lonely.

"Look at that," Iggy said, "wouldn't it be cool."

He was pointing at an obviously handmade pair of overalls and shirt that hung on a gigantic plaster mannequin.

"People like to see the clothes," Ben was saying. He was talking to Mom and Dad as they wandered into the gallery. "It gives them a better sense of size than from photographs.

You're seeing it life size, the way it was worn. That's different from looking at a little picture."

"If I got that big," Iggy told her, "nobody would ever bother me again. It would be so much fun."

She tuned him out and went back to the pictures. The Peter in the pictures wasn't having fun. In the newspaper articles, they always had him standing with normal sized people, or holding normal sized objects, like books or tools, to emphasize his size. He looked shy and embarrassed.

It must have been awful, she thought suddenly. His size made him alone. He couldn't play regular games or do regular things. He couldn't even go out on dates or wear ordinary clothes.

Nobody would understand, she thought suddenly, they'd look at him like Iggy did, and think it was good to be so big. They wouldn't realize how lonely he was as his body changed. They wouldn't realize how trapped he would feel in his body, how foreign and strange it would seem to him.

She knew what that was like. She'd felt her breasts ache as they'd grown. Had felt a strange self-consciousness about them, proud and ashamed at the same time, sometimes wishing they were gone, sometimes proud of their evidence of her womanhood. Wendy had marked the growth of body hair, and the thickening of her hips, and even menstruation with nervous, frightened anticipation.

"He was shaving three times a day, by this time," she overheard Ben say.

She looked again at the photographs. Yes, you could see the five o'clock shadows in the pictures.

There were more changes; the eyebrows had become heavier, bushier, giving him a vaguely sinister appearance. They gradually grew together. His features became blunter through the series of pictures. The brows and neck grew heavier, his hands became spadelike. The figure in the photographs seemed much older, perhaps thirties or forties, with the heaviness of middle age. Only his eyes seemed young.

She looked away from the pictures, staring instead at grossly oversized sneakers. She could put both her feet into one, she thought to herself.

"I mean," Ben was telling her Dad, "if your son is big, you're proud, you know. It's good to have a tall kid, a heavyweight. It means that he'll probably be good at sports and stuff. He'll be strong."

"And then one day, you realize he's seven feet tall and still growing, and it's not good anymore. Clothes don't fit, and shoes need to be custom made. He can't sit on most furniture."

"Originally we thought he was just a giant," Ben said. "We worried about it though. There could be health complications if he got too big. Even if there weren't, where would he find a job? What about clothes? Or a car? What would he do for furniture?"

"I didn't want my boy to be a freak."

He laughed.

"Funny the things that occupy your time. As it turned out, none of that stuff mattered."

"Robert Wadlow, remember him? Before Peter, he'd been the tallest man in the world. He'd died of complications of a foot infection. A foot infection of all things."

"You're worried about him getting sick, like Wadlow. Being so big, he can't properly stand or run or walk. You start to worry about him falling down and breaking something, or having a heart attack, because his heart just can't take the strain..."

The last picture showed Peter barefoot in nothing but a pair of briefs, surrounded by men in white coats. He'd tried to smile for the camera. His body was covered with matted hair.

"That was when we started taking him to Doctors..."

Wendy followed them into the next gallery.

"And the problem was," Ben was saying, "as it turned out, there was nothing wrong with him. He was just growing up, and it was the rest of us that weren't."

"We tried to make allowances as best we could. We wanted Peter to have as close to a normal life as we could. So we built this for him..."

Ben opened a door.

"Peter's cottage," Ben announced proudly.

They stepped, through a narrow hallway, out of what Wendy judged to be the house proper, and into the barn that had been beside the house.

"Wow," Dad said, obviously pleased, "this is amazing. Did you do this yourself?"

"Some," the man admitted. "The cottage building itself, and mainly the furniture."

Everything in the room was outrageously oversized, built for a giant. It wasn't just huge; it was massive, everything conveying the feeling of weight and solidity.

Wendy didn't like it; it made her feel like a little kid, dwarfed by her surroundings. As she walked by a chair whose seat came up to her chest, its wooden legs were massive out of proportion to the chair, they were pillars like an elephants legs. Standing she couldn't even see the top of the table.

Iggy scampered up what looked like a high chair with laddered steps that had obviously been made to allow normal sized humans to sit at the table

There was a titanic sofa chair, and a dreadnought sized couch. She reached up to feel the arm of the plush covering. The couch and chair faced a television set. It was the only thing that didn't give her vertigo. It was huge, a seventy-five inch monster, but you could find them that big in any department store.

The remote was a black slab a foot long, with red rubber buttons the size of the tip of her thumb. She recognized the buttons suddenly as India rubber erasers, like the ones from school, which had been carved into shape.

In one corner was a computer. It had a massive twenty four inch screen and an outrageous three and a half foot long keyboard.

In the other corner, next to the wooden table and chairs was the kitchenette, again, with ludicrously oversized stove and fridge.

"Hey guys," Iggy called, from atop the table, he held up a cup the size of a small bucket.

"Get down from there," Dad called, scandalized. He turned to the man.

"I'm sorry Ben, you know how kids are."

"It's okay," Ben said. "I just wouldn't want him to get hurt up there."

"Come down or else," Mom ordered.

"Aww," Iggy said, as he clambered down onto one of the high chairs. He descended its steps.

What a hyperactive little creep, Wendy thought. Wasn't he ever going to grow up?

Ben led them into the final gallery. The lasts gasps of the Sasquatch Kid museum. It was a long narrow room with a series of displays, culminating in the entrance to the gift shop.

"Hell of a place," Dad said. "Did he ever live there?"

"No," Ben admitted, "not really. I mean, he'd look at the stuff, as we got it, or as we built it, and you could tell he was impressed."

There was a final display of home photographs. Peter now, mostly naked but for breeches; body completely hairy. Totally huge. You could see how he towered over his surroundings. His frame had filled out, giving him massive solidity.

There was a life sized composite photograph. A little card announced that at the time of his last measurement, Peter had stood eleven feet, ten inches tall. Beside the poster was a plaster cast of his foot.

Another little card announced that Sasquatch sightings over the world varied from five to nine feet or greater. In North America, the average was eight feet. But in the British Columbia Rockies, individuals as tall as fifteen feet had been reported.

"But mainly, he seemed to prefer sleeping outdoors. He appreciated it, the house and the stuff we built for him, but it was like he'd gone beyond having a use for it."

The next display was the Sasquatch Kid TV movie. Copies of stills and promotional materials. A seven foot tall black basketball player had played Peter. The costume hung in a display case. It seemed small, compared to Peter's real things. The card next to the costume indicated that the actor had eventually died of AIDS.

Another card told her that the TV movie had been a pilot, but that the network had decided not to go ahead with a TV series.

"Looking back," Ben said, "I think what we were trying to do was to cling to an illusion of normality. He was still our Peter, just bigger. That wasn't true. He was growing up."

"I know what you mean," Dad said. "I remember when Wendy and Iggy were both in diapers. Sometimes it's hard to realize..."

"No," said Ben, "it was more than that. I mean, you've got good kids. But they'll grow up to be like us. Peter didn't."

"You've got to understand...a lot of what we are, exists because in some fundamental ways, we don't grow up. We're stuck as perpetual infants, needing to be taken care of all our lives. We can't survive out there on our own."

"That's why we make clothes, and houses, and all these other things. Because we need them. Peter didn't need them."

"But it's more than that. It has to do with thinking. Look at people, aren't we all just monkeys...permanent kids? Always exploring, fascinated by new things, puzzles and tools, emotionally volatile. Even language, at its most fundamental level, is just chattering for mommy."

"As Peter grew...matured; his mind, his outlook changed. He just didn't think about things the same way that we did. He was intelligent enough; he scored high on tests, when he bothered to take them."

"But he just got less and less interested in toys...in houses and clothes, in cars and videos and school."

"Slowly he stopped wearing clothes. He slept outdoors, even in bad weather. He'd go out on these long walks into the woods. Sometimes for days."

The next display was a map designating the 'Sasquatch Kid Federal Wildlife Reserve,' the government had bought up all the lands surrounding the town, to give Peter a place to live wild.

"He spoke less and less."

"One day, we were out sitting together on the porch, watching the sunset, and I asked him. I said 'Peter, you don't talk much anymore?'"

"He thought about it for a while. We just sat there together and watched the sun set. Then he put his arm around me and held me close, kind of like you'd do with your own child, and by that time I wasn't much bigger than your boy there, compared to him.

"Finally, he cleared his throat, and he said, pronouncing each word carefully, like he knew it was going to be his last, 'most things don't need to be said.'

"That was the last time anyone ever heard him speak."

The next display was about the Sasquatch researchers. The men and women who followed Peter around, collecting his stools, noting his footprints. Occasionally catching glimpses of him.

Next to it was a display of Sasquatches around the world. A large map of the world with clusters of sightings here and there. The display announced that there might be as many as three hundred Sasquatch living in a world with six billion people.

There was a moment of uncomfortable silence as they digested that. Ben Winston looked small and lonely.

"One day, he turned eighteen, and just walked out there, into the woods. That was the last time I saw him."

There was an uncomfortable silence, even Iggy was quiet.

Dad looked around, almost fidgeting and spoke.

"Well, Ben, I've got to thank you for sharing that with us, but we've got some miles to travel before we can rest, so I guess we'd better get going."

The next to last display was simply a montage of photographs, grainy, blurry images of Peter taken in the wild. Names and dates under them. In the middle of it all was a couple of framed newspaper clippings.

"Peter Winston shot!" a local headline blared. Early one morning Peter had simply walked into town to the local clinic, startling the paperboy and the early risers. He had patiently waited for the Doctor to show up and take two .22 bullets out of his shoulder. Then, when the wound was sutured and antibiotics administered, he'd calmly stood and walked out of town. He'd been gone by the time his father arrived.

There were a few follow up articles: Researchers announced that they'd found no evidence of human remains in Peter's stools. No suspects were ever located. A law was passed declaring any attempt to kill or injure a Sasquatch to be a death penalty offence.

Wendy stared at the photographs. She could tell Peter didn't like to be photographed any more. The blurred grainy shots were all the pictures there would be of him. He was, she thought, terribly unutterably isolated and alone. Tears welled in her eyes, it was so tragic.

"I want to get a T-Shirt," Iggy screeched, bouncing into the gift shop, shattering her moment.

In the end, they all bought T-Shirts, and posters, and postcards, and a little Sasquatch Kid doll that looked suspiciously, to Wendy, like the Wookie from Star Wars. Mom bought a copy of the Sasquatch Kid TV movie Blu-ray, and another documentary DVD called "The Real Sasquatch Kid." Wendy bought a book, "Sasquatch" by Rene Dahinden, "a special updated edition." There were a few chapters on Peter.

Dad seemed to have lost the sombre mood that had accompanied the end of Ben's story. Instead, he and Iggy got into the T-Shirts right away, changing in the bathroom. Then they'd insisted that Wendy and her mother change. Wendy complied with poor grace.

Then there were the endless photographs, with Ben, without Ben, with the giant ugly statue. With some of the nick-knacks from Peters cottage.

Wendy found herself growing steadily more irritated. Men were retarded apes. Suddenly, watching Dad, she could believe it. Balding, grey hair, potbelly and all, in his spoiled enthusiasm, he reminded her a lot of Iggy.

Finally, it was over. Just as they were getting in the car, Dad stopped and impulsively hugged Iggy. Wendy watched from the other side of the car. And then they were on the road again.

"How much time did we lose?" Dad asked.

"An hour and three quarters," Mom told him.

"Not too bad," Dad said.

They drove down the highway. Beside the road, there were occasional signs announcing that the area was a wildlife sanctuary.

"No reason for it, you know," Dad said softly to no one in particular. "It just sort of happened. Could have happened to anyone."

Wendy thought about alleles and genetic off and on switches.

A sign announced "Caidinville, three miles. Food and Gas."

"Hey," Wendy said, feeling cramps starting again.

"Hmm," Dad replied.

"I have to go to the bathroom," she said.

"When?"

"Soon."

"For Christ's sake, Wendy, you were just in the bathroom at the museum," Dad said irritably.

"But I didn't go."

"And whose fault is that?" he asked.

"I didn't need to go then," she replied.

"I have to go too," Iggy said.

"We can stop at the next gas station, and pick up gas as well dear," Mom said. "It won't take more than ten minutes."

"Fine," Dad sulked, "it's a wonder we get anywhere."

They pulled into the gas station. Dad picked up the washroom keys for both kids. He made a point of saying that he didn't need to go himself. He'd gone at the museum.

The bathroom was out back. Wendy locked herself in the dingy bathroom. Hurriedly she squatted, hovering above the toilet and then changed her pads, dumping the old one in the garbage can under the sink.

Men just didn't understand about these things, she thought bitterly to herself. In the bathroom, the reek of her own menstruation was suffocating.

As she stepped out of the door, she saw something from the corner of her eye, and there he was.

At first, her mind locked up, refusing to comprehend. Even the life size composite photograph hadn't readied her for the size of the being beside her, the solid physical massiveness of it. It took an instant for her mind to break it down into arms and legs, torso, face, hands, feet. A huge body covered with shaggy brown hair.

"Holy shit," she whispered. How had it gotten so close?

It was staring at her. Under the warm brown eyes, its nostrils flared, and she could hear a soft snorting as it inhaled.

It's Peter, she thought. It's the Sasquatch Kid.

He...it...lifted a long log of an arm, reaching out to her. Her eyes followed it. Was he going to shake hands? She wondered. She felt paralysed, unable to move, barely able to breathe.

The immense finger, thick and heavy prodded softly at her T-shirt, sending odd sensations through her pert breasts. Her nipples hardened almost painfully, sticking up against the fabric.

"Oh God! I'm getting felt up by Bigfoot." She blushed as the almost surreal thought coursed through her head.

But almost as soon as she had the thought, she realized that he was just tracing the outline of his own face on her "Sasquatch Kid" T-shirt.

That realization gave her the strength to lift her eyes up along the length of immense hairy arm, all the way to the huge head and shoulders gazing down at her: Staring at his own image.

At least, she hoped that was all he was doing.

It's all right, she told herself. It's all right.

"You're Peter, aren't you?"

Wendy was glad she'd been to the museum after all. She was dead certain that she would have screamed or fainted or done the absolutely wrong thing otherwise. The museum had allowed her to become used to the concept. To the idea of someone or something like Peter.

There was no sign of recognition of the name. It simply continued to gently move its finger along the image on her T-Shirt, prodding her breasts.

Her stomach tightened. Maybe it's not Peter. Maybe it's another one. A dangerous one. Her heart, already racing, felt like it shifted gears, cardiac afterburners about to kick in with nitro.

She tried to force herself to calm down. It wasn't doing anything hostile. Not really.

Wendy forced herself to look at it carefully. She felt like she was in a state of heightened awareness. She felt the pebbles under her sandals and the sweat pooling at the small of her back. She felt like she could count the hairs on its arms, they were so vivid and distinct.

She looked into its face. Calm blue eyes looking back at her.

It was Peter, she decided. She looked down, at what would have been eye level for her.

She was only vaguely aware of the difference between flaccid and erect, but she was suddenly, totally certain that she was staring at the largest penis she was ever going to see in her lifetime, as it hung there, dangling down between hair legs thick as tree trunks.

It twitched.

Wendy inhaled rasping, she couldn't get enough of a breath. Her heart, already pounding, felt like it was going to punch out of her chest as her stomach did cartwheels.

She desperately wanted to scream, but she couldn't seem to get enough of a breath. All she could manage was a series of rasping wheezes. Her whole body seemed to go slick with sweat and her nostrils filled with the scent of her own desperate agitation.

The creature's nostrils flared again, it stared into her face, withdrawing its hand from her chest.

It smells me, she thought, it smells my body, my womb, my female hormones. It's going to carry me off and rape me.

It crouched down, almost on its knees, and still seemed to tower over her. It put a huge hand on her shoulder, but she didn't feel its weight, just a kind of warm presence and began to make a soft rumbling soothing sound in the back of its throat.

Wendy thought she would fall down, but to her surprise, she didn't. Her mind, her body, which had felt like a roller coaster out of control, began to slow down. Gradually, she decided that it wasn't going to do anything.

Perhaps it had been attracted to her, to her smell, to the scent of a young girl in puberty, to the odour of hormones going wild, transforming her body. Perhaps that was why it was here. But it wasn't going to do anything. She was too young.

As far as it... As far as Peter was concerned, she was just a child, and she would always be one. Her scent might have called to him, but she wasn't what he wanted or needed.

Peter took his hand off her shoulder and stepped back. Rearing to his full height, he blocked out the sun. She was awed by the immensity of him.

"My name is Wendy," she told him, "like in the book." She blushed, feeling impossibly stupid at such a lame thing to say.

Peter grinned at her words, his smile a rare and impossible thing. For him, she realized, he lived in a world of children who would never grow up.

That was why his people had vanished, had retreated to hiding places and secret groves. The world had been inherited by children, who'd filled it up and pushed them out, and they'd never had the heart to push back.

He bowed down.

His breath stank and she closed her eyes, heart starting to race again in terror.

She felt something rubbery brush her forehead.

A kiss.

When she opened her eyes, Peter was striding calmly away. She watched his round buttocks moving smoothly as he reached the forest in three strides, and vanished in two more.

Peter was gone.

Wendy stood there, uncertain of what to do. The bathroom door opened behind her.

Iggy stepped out of the men's room.

"What are you standing there for?" he asked impatiently, irritated by the thought that she might have been waiting for him.

"Let's get going," he said.

She looked down at the ground, where Peter had walked off. There in a patch of soft earth, a dozen feet away, was a footprint.

Proof of her adventure?

She could show it to Iggy, he'd be thrilled. She could show it to Mom and Dad, and tell them the story.

She stared at the woods.

Maybe not.

"Let's get going," she said.

The End

Tell Me

In spite of the traces of mascara, darkening his eyes, he looked like a thirteen year old boy. No thirteen year old should be hanging around on streets like these at this time of night. I pulled over and unlocked my door.

He read me as soon as he got in, I could see it in his eyes.

"Wanna drive around?" he asked, staying in character.

"I have a place." I told him, playing along. I pressed a stud, the doors locked. He was trapped.

"Oh," he said, "okay." He leaned back in the seat, displaying an apparent apathetic lack of interest. Underneath the veneer, I could sense him, like electricity, looking desperately for a way out.

"Put on your seat belt." I told him.

"Okay," he said, shouldering into it, "just don't hurt me. Okay?"

He tried to catch my eyes with a lost pleading look.

"It's all over." I told him. I didn't bother looking at him, I wasn't that stupid.

I drove to the place. He watched the streets through the car windows as we passed. A parade of winos and pimps, hookers of both sexes and any age. Even kids. Like he pretended to be.

"I'll never see this again, will I?" he said wistfully.

"No." I answered.

We didn't say anything for the rest of the trip.

The place was a fifth rate hotel still on the downhill slide. The neighborhood was so bombed out that not even street trash with any sense or self-respect would come here. It was the refuge of the dregs of the dregs. The hotel had been placarded with so many health notices, and municipal standards violations that it had ceased to be even marginally profitable. It was about to disappear into an endless succession of shell corporations, while squatters and schizophrenics took over the sagging remnants of the physical structure.

I figured it was far enough outside his territory that he wouldn't sense me preparing it. He'd been cagey. For a solid month I'd cruised the streets, daylight glinting off my hood, looking for him, hoping to find him sleeping in his lair. He'd hidden himself damned well. Had that been because of me? I wondered. Or was it just some inbuilt paranoia?

I couldn't tell from looking at him. But then, I didn't suppose it mattered. Eventually, I'd had to come searching for him at night. I'd prepared.

I pulled up in a narrow alleyway behind the hotel, directly opposite its back door.

I got out of the car first, taking the keys and locking the door behind me. Not that it mattered, he couldn't get out, and it wasn't as if he'd be able to drive away.

I walked around to the passenger's side. I opened the door for him.

The minute he got out he tried to turn to mist and slither away beneath the car. I'd loaded the undercarriage with garlic. It stopped him.

I waited patiently as he reformed himself into a retching fetal ball. I reached into my pocket and turned off the cars internal UV screens. It wasn't necessary now.

He climbed to his feet, looking small and battered. I suppressed an urge to help him. Was this how he had claimed his victims? Playing on fugitive sympathies?

He looked around. The walls were covered with Hex symbols, painted with spray cans and looking like graffiti. Not really harmful to him, unless he tried to climb the walls. The way back was soaked with dried garlic residues, he'd have an easier time walking over burning coals.

He looked at the narrow slash of sky, shining down into the alley. You could just make out a crescent moon. I could tell he just wanted to shift out and fly away. But he could sense the wards I'd installed so carefully up there. He'd never make it the UV lamps would catch him in the air with no place to hide. He'd come burning down to earth, and I'd end him.

"Time to go," I told him, unlocking the back door. I'd been doing this for six years now, there were no more mistakes left to make.

"Why are you doing this?" he asked forlornly.

I thought of Lenore, poor lost Lenore. I hardened my heart,

I didn't owe him an answer. I didn't owe any of them an answer.

"It's time." I said.

For a moment he stiffened. Almost ready to attack, I could see it in him. But then he relaxed. I was much too well protected, any direct assault on me would be fatal. Otherwise he would have tried it in the car.

The only place he could go was through the door. I followed him, sealing it behind me.

He walked up to the third floor, before turning down the hall because he couldn't go any higher. He was alert for the slightest opportunity, but there weren't any.

I was right behind him.

Halfway down he stopped in front of the room, unable to go any further but unwilling to enter voluntarily. I opened the door for him.

He stepped inside, looking around as he did so. It was a tiny hotel room, barely larger than a janitor's closet. I flicked the light, roaches scurried across worn floorboards to hide under a threadbare cot. There was a leaking sink in one corner, a few feet down from it, a rickety chair and something that might have been called a writing desk. There were no windows.

He sat down on the cot.

"I know this place," he told me, "it's just like every other place."

I sealed the door.

"I was born in 1550 in Florence," he said, "I knew Michelangelo. He loved me."

I sat down in the chair. Looking at him.

"That's not true," he admitted after a moment.

He looked up at me. What part wasn't true, I wondered. That he was 400 years old from Italy? That he'd known Michelangelo? Or that Michelangelo had told him that he loved him?

None of it mattered to me, not after Lenore.

"I knew you'd come for me. Especially after Sebastian."

Sebastian had damned near killed me. He had been the first to come looking for me. In the end, Sebastian had died. He hadn't been the first, nor would this one be the last.

It continued to be a source of vague surprise that they talked to each other; they shared information somehow. Each one of them had struck me as solitary and uncommunicative. When not hunting for victims, they had been totally apathetic.

Still, child molesters talked to each other. And serial killers. So why not? Birds of a feather flocked together; why not vampires of a line?

"It's over," I told him, "nothing you can say, nothing you can do, will make a difference."

He nodded.

"I don't remember my mother," he said softly, "or any family at all. I don't remember anything except being alone and lonely, and the men. Even when I was alive, that was all there was. Just emptiness and the men who came and went. There were men who said they were my friends, and there were men who said they loved me. But after they had what they wanted, they would go."

"It was no different afterwards. I still let them do what they wanted. Sometimes, I would ask them to tell me that they loved me."

"And if they didn't?" I asked.

"I would kill them." For the first time I saw the flash of his fangs.

What generations of monsters he'd created. I thought. I'd wondered, as I'd tracked them down and killed them, where had they all come from. What fiend had empowered them?

He was just a victim, a particular kind of victim who attracted a particular kind of bastard. In death, in undeath, he'd gone on being a victim, attracting the same kind of bastards, making them immortal.

It made a perverse kind of sense.

They all seemed kind of pathetic to me. Not what you would expect from immortal bloodthirsty monsters. They were not operatic figures. They were just tired listless parodies of themselves, going through the motions. Hollow copies of whoever, whatever they'd been in life.

"Listen," I said to him, "you ever hear of reincarnation?"

His look was meaningless.

"Some believe that you get born over and over. You die and get reborn, right. The wheel of reincarnation. It's so you learn. You change from one incarnation to the next. Getting better. So you don't have to keep making the same mistakes over and over again."

I made a motion with my hand.

"Maybe it's right, maybe it's wrong. But you...people, it's like you get off the wheel. You don't go anywhere. You just keep doing things over and over again. You're like a scratched record, jumping in the same groove all the time."

"Maybe you can get back on the wheel. Maybe you can make it change." Did he understand me? There was no way to tell, looking at those lost and guarded eyes.

I don't know why I tried to offer this one a fugitive bit of comfort. I'd never done it for any of the others. I had never even thought in those terms before. I momentarily considered letting him go, but then I thought of Lenore.

No.

He nodded. He stood up and shimmied out of his jeans. He pulled his T-Shirt over his head. Naked, he laid face down on the worn blankets of the cot. His head was turned away from me, facing the wall, cradled in his arms.

"This way." he said.

I took out the hammer and stake, crossed over to him. He did not move. The cot springs creaked with my weight as I positioned myself over him.

Like a broken record, trapped in its groove. I thought.

His unnatural flesh squirmed slightly as I positioned the stake just off the spinal column, between two ribs. There were tears in my eyes.

"Tell me you love me," he whispered.

I swing the hammer.

The End

Skin

"At first," I tell the policeman, "I was afraid that I was going to be raped. Then I was terrified that he was going to kill me. As it turned out, it was much worse than that."

"But I'm getting ahead of myself."

&&&

Nothing especially bad had ever happened to me. Bad things had happened to people that I knew, and I certainly read about it in the news. Still, I had no expectation that it would ever happen to me. Not if I was careful and stayed out of trouble.

I guess we all have the expectation that we can avoid it. It won't happen to us. We'll be careful; we'll take the right vitamins, or do push ups, or say our prayers. Maybe we just believe we're invulnerable or blessed. Nothing bad will ever happen to me. I just can't imagine it. Just won't allow it.

Bad things are like an earthquake. It just happens. That's all.

&&&

I sit in the examining room of the Emergency ward, a blood stained blanket wrapped around my naked body.

The nurse doesn't much like it. Too bad. She keeps giving me looks, like she was trying to figure the best way to get the blanket away from me.

"We'll get you a gown," the Doctor says. He'd finished his examination; they've cleaned the excess blood off and applied liniments and antibiotics.

"How are you?" the policeman asks me. "Injuries?"

"It's all right," I tell him vaguely. For some reason, it's hard to pay attention. "Just superficial cuts, scratches really.

They bled a lot. But they're not bleeding now. They just tingle."

Part of me isn't in the room with him. My mind is elsewhere, still back there.

"I thought he was going to skin me. I thought he was going to skin me alive."

"How did you get away?" he asks.

"I have a dislocated thumb," I say. "I got it playing softball when I was fifteen. It's more a pain in the ass than anything else."

"There was a noise outside. He went to check on it or something. He left his knife behind, right in front of me. My wrists were tied down, but I managed to slip my hand free because of my thumb. I grabbed the knife, and cut myself loose. Then I got out of there and started running down the highway."

Four cars passed a naked screaming blood covered woman staggering down the highway before one stopped to help.

Says something about humanity, doesn't it?

"How did it happen?" he says.

I start to tell him about my day. I am like a robot, just spewing events out, from the start, without discrimination. I tell him about breakfast. About work and lunch. About my plans for the evening.

About being grabbed by a smooth voiced Latino male who called himself Juan. About how I'd thought it was just a mugging at first, except Juan wanted me to go with him.

I talk about terror and helplessness. I'd felt powerless and paralysed, mind racing in horrified overdrive, as he took me to a shed and tied me spread eagled to a concrete floor.

I tell him about the chants and the dance. The candles that he lit. And the chalk circles he'd marked out around me.

He'd gagged me and cut off my clothes off with his knife.

Then he'd started to cut me, all the time whispering soft reassurances.

I can't breathe suddenly. I start to gasp. The policeman looks upset, like he should do something but doesn't know what.

The Doctor puts his arm around my shoulder.

"It's all right," he says softly.

It isn't all right. It is never going to be all right. But I get my breathing under control.

"Do you want to stay overnight," the Doctor asks. "For observation, just to make sure you'll be safe."

"No," I say. This is a strange place, not safe. I want to go back to where I am safe. "I want to go home."

&&&

The police officers take me home. Just to be safe, they inspect the apartment for me, checking for rapists under the bed and inside the cupboard. They leave me their cards, plain white squares with matter of fact black printing. Names and phone numbers. Just the facts, Ma'am.

I sit in my living room, wrapped in my Sears' terrycloth bathrobe, holding a cup of coffee. The robe golden brown and two sizes two big, and it always leaves me feeling secure, like a little girl in daddy's arms.

I have no taste for the coffee. No urge to drink. It's hot, and the flavour is the same, but there's no satisfaction. It slowly grows cold in my hands as I watch television classics. Jerry Seinfeld gives way to Ellen, which turns into ancient Miami Vice reruns, the then another cop show, and finally the late movie.

The channel goes dead. I find another television station that is still running and watch "I Love Lucy" while the sun comes up.

I draw the curtains, darkening the apartment. Briefly I contemplate putting blankets up over the windows. But I know that's insane.

I decide to take a bath. I've always loved baths. There's nothing like climbing into a hot tub and letting your cares float away.

&&&

I have a dream. I am lying in the tub, letting the hot water sooth my tension away, when I notice a piece of plastic floating on the water.

I stare at it, affectlessly, for a few moments. Watching it without special interest. It looks like a glove. A soft pink glove.

It is attached to my shoulder.

The skin of my hand and arm has slipped off my body. It floats there, bobbing against my breasts in the bathtub.

Suddenly, in the tub I am very cold. My breath catches in my throat and I am caught between the powerful urge to vomit and scream simultaneously.

I do neither.

With my free hand, I carefully pick up the skin of my other hand. It hangs there, limply across my fingers, like a pink glove. I stare at the detail of fingernails and knuckles, tiny hairs and lines. It is slightly thick, thicker farther up the arm, from subcutaneous fat deposits under the skin. That's why it floats, occurs to me with a tormented rationality.

My other arm sits there under the water, an unfeeling construct of bone and grey tendons, red muscle, laced with blood vessels. There is a fundamentally unsettling feeling at looking at these parts of yourself

With exceeding care, I slide the skin back onto the arm. My fingers flexing as the skin fastens back onto them.

&&&

It wasn't a dream.

My skin keeps slipping off.

I call my Doctor. He tells me that it can't possibly happen and that I might be experiencing a stress reaction, or possibly I was reacting badly to tranquillizers.

I haven't taken any sedatives. The little plastic bottle sits unopened in the kitchen. I don't know if I should tell him that..

He schedules me for an appointment.

My skin keeps slipping off.

There is a bad smell in the apartment, like something is rotting.

I can feel Juan out there, somewhere.

&&&

At 10:00 A.M., I return to the place it happened. I wear a red skirt and jacket with black pantyhose. I have a butcher knife in my purse, and a can of mace in my hands.

I know that if I look in a mirror, I would look just like I looked yesterday. Or last week. Or last month.

But it's not the same.

Everything is different now, and I don't know why. I want to be my old self. I want to think my old thoughts. I want to be able to curl up with my teddy bear, and love banana sundaes and sad movies, and go to parties.

I use bandaids to tape my skin together, along my back and wrists, wherever it parts. I run out of bandaids. After that, I use scotch tape and then electrical tape. I make glossy black X's of tape up my legs and down my arms. It's almost like a sexy fetish look, but I don't find it funny. My skin sweats and the tape wants to lift, so I have to keep pressing it back in place.

I stand outside the door. I remember escaping, the morning light as I stumbled away. How long had I been in there?. I should run away again, but I don't.

The door swings open.

It's just an old tool shed, tin and planks leaning against a larger building, no longer in use. Not worth the trouble of tearing down. I step under the police line.

The light is poor. The chalked circle is washed away. Why would they do that? The eye hooks are still there, driven into the concrete. There are still stains on the ground. Blood. Urine. Shit. Me.

I start to shake, violently. My nose is running. Juan is somewhere in his mind. I remember the things he said, in his soft whispering voices. The promises he made as he tied me to the floor even though neither of us really believed them. I remember the gag, some piece of salty old leather, cutting into my jaws. I remember him cutting with the knife....

Abruptly, I am outside again. The sun shines, beating down on me. That familiar sensation, the urgent need to

Giant Monsters Sing Sad Songs / **Page 55**

scream and vomit comes pushing up my throat. I take a breath and do neither.

I feel like I'm standing outside, watching myself. I feel like I'm going through the motions of emotions. Am I still in shock?

The knife.

I can feel it.

I look around, staring at industrial decay, crumbling concrete, weeds, arcane rusting ironwork.

There.

I see a glimmer, buried in weeds a dozen feet away. Why didn't the police find it? Crossing over to it I kneel and part the weeds. There are dried brown spots near the handle. My blood?

The blade is rose coloured and nearly translucent; it is roughly serrated, as if it was chipped into shape. The handle is covered with little rings of light coloured leather.

Reaching in my purse, I pick it up with tissue papers and deposit it inside. It seems to pull in my hands.

The pieces of tape holding my skin together in back, part as I bend over. I feel my skin sliding loosely, hanging off my shoulders. Only my bra and pantyhose keeps it from spilling completely. My guts twist inside me, as if they are loose too. I feel like I'm coming apart.

I sense...recognition in the knife.

As if it knows me.

I don't have a sense of it being alive. Whatever this thing is, it's just inanimate. Just a tool. But there's some shell of awareness inside it. It recognizes me, it pulls, the way iron recognizes and pulls to magnets.

It was waiting for Juan to come back for it. But Juan was cautious, and I've found it first.

Inside my purse, it touches the butcher knife, and steel curdles.

What in hell is this thing?

What the hell am I doing?

&&&

I was going to take the knife to the police. Walk in, leave them with the evidence. See if they could lift prints from it.

On the way over, I drive past a New Age Shop. Cosmic Crystals the sign says. I pull in.

Why not a magic shop?

Juan was trying to do sorcery. He'd made his circle in the ground, done his chants, spilled my blood. Maybe they can tell me what it was all about.

I don't believe it, of course. Not really. Juan was crazy, and I'm experiencing some sort of delayed stress reaction. It happens. But maybe they can tell me something and I can start putting myself together.

Or maybe they'll just feed this chain reaction of delusions I'm having. I don't know.

As I stand in front of the door, I do know that doing something is better than doing nothing. That if I allow myself to go home and put blankets up over my windows, it won't end there. I'll keep retreating and retreating inside myself until there's no place left to be.

The door jingles as I walk in. The air is thick with incense.

My foot burns for a second.

I look down. How odd. Someone's left a line of salt and greasy grey dust in the doorway.

There are shelves of handmade jewelry in cases. Books and paraphernalia. The titles announce themselves: Improve your love life, improve your sex life, find the perfect partner, discover past existences, or future powers. I'm not interested.

"Yes," comes a voice, the accent is thick, French and Caribbean. Haitian?

A heavy black woman comes out from curtains and stands in front of a glass counter.

"I have something to show you," I tell her, walking to the counter, holding my purse in front of me. "Do you know anything about this?"

Still holding the knife in tissues, I take it out of the purse and lay it on the counter.

She looks at it and then at me.

"It's obsidian," she says. "Volcanic rock. Like those chimes there."

She indicates with a nod. I turn briefly to look at a set of door chimes that appears to have been made for Fred Flintstone.

"...flint," she is saying. "Indians used to chip it into arrowheads and blades. The Aztecs would make it into knives and use it to skin their sacrifices."

"Why?" I ask, it might be a clue.

She shrugs. "Who knows? Bad things, certainly."

She touches it and then jerks her hand back like it was red hot. She looks shocked. Not just surprised, frightened.

"That's your blood on it, isn't it?" she asks, as if it's my fault.

"Yes."

"Get out!" she says. She looks angry, like she's going to spit at me.

"What?" I am shocked by her reaction. It frightens me.

"Get out now!"

"Why?"

"Because I don't want nothing to do with that. Or with you."

"What is it?"

"It's bad, and I want nothing to do with it."

"I'm in trouble," I tell her desperately.

"Yes you are," she says. "But I can't help you."

"Please," I beg.

In the end, she sells me a charm on a rawhide cord for $29.99. It won't solve my problems, she tells me. But it may help make a difference at the right moment. I wear it around my neck, it nestles between my breasts. In my imagination, it feels warm.

Outside the store, I feel the knife pulling again in my purse. Somewhere out there, I can sense Juan.

Surrendering to the inevitable, I begin to follow it.

&&&

Once I give in to the pull, I find its home quickly.

Giant Monsters Sing Sad Songs / **Page 58**

The twitchy feeling of presence that I had come to think of as Juan isn't here. Just the pull of the knife..

I take out my Visa and begin to jimmy the door like I've seen in movies. It opens almost immediately, as if it was waiting for me all along, as if it wants to open for me.

The door yawns wide open. I stare.

It seems so ordinary. Like anyone's living room. There is a television set, an old DVD player, ratty but comfortable looking old furniture. There is a small stack of magazines on the coffee table.

With palpable effort, I take a breath and step inside.

It still feels ordinary.

Fine. A nice ordinary home. Too ordinary. The relentless normality is too perfect. It feels like a dusty veneer. Like a hotel room that no one has stayed in for a long time.

There has to be something more.

I step into the hallway. That too is ordinary.

Off the hallway, there's a room full of dressers and bureaus. Clothes of every sort hang in profusion. Odd perhaps. But not weird with capital letters.

The last room.

That isn't ordinary, not ordinary at all.

It had been a bedroom, but there was no bed, anymore.

The carpeting has been taken up. In the rough wood of the floor is a crudely drawn circle, bordered by arcane symbols.

I step into the room, one wall is a walk in closet. On either side are two dressers.

There is an altar on one of them. A crowded profusion of small bones, feathers, pots and candles.

The knife hums in my purse as I approach the altar. As if it knows it's coming home.

Something in the corner, brownish pink and shapeless, caught my eye.

I walk over to it. At first my mind refuses to grasp it. I couldn't, wouldn't absorb it. It looks like a rumpled paper bag, or maybe a pile of rubber or plastic.

It is a skin.

It can't be.

With a bone from the altar, I reach down and poke it, stretch it, turn it over and spread it out a little.

It's Juan.

Or at least, it's his skin.

Dumbly I stare at it, trying to comprehend. To imagine what happened to him.

Had he been an agent of some mad skinning cult? And when he failed to bring back a victim, they had turned on him?

It writhes suddenly, a sensuous animal ripple that slides across its's flat limp surface. I jump back.

It's still again. Had I imagined it?

No. There's a dead certainty in me that it is still alive. That if I touch it, it will be warm, it will curl around my hand; that it will flatly writhe to embrace me, wrap its contours around my body...

Stop.

Leave, I tell myself. Turn around and get the hell out of here before whatever it is that lives here comes back. Turn around and walk out, and for the rest of my life, never ever look back.

No.

Look in the closet, something urges me.

Look in the closet and then I can get the hell out of there.

Yes.

Two quick steps forward, and I fling the closet doors wide open.

It is full of naked human skins hanging limp on wire coat hangers.

White ones, black ones, dusky skins. Men's skins, women's skins, breasts and genitals protruding uselessly. The dried skins nestled one another.

I stare in mounting paralysed horror.

Some are very very fresh. Others were old. Unbearably old. Worn through in places old. Falling apart old.

He doesn't wear those outside, I thought. He keeps them for inside. He wears them until they fall apart. And he always wants more.

Individual shapes became apparent. And more. There are what looked like dog's skins. Wolves? Some fresh, some very old. Is that a bear? Another, an orangutan?

There are children's skins in there.

What kind of madman is this?

The most horrible part is the growing certainty, that they are all still somehow alive. Suddenly, I'm certain that they are all aware of me.

Somehow, I know that if I touch one, I'll be able to breathe its memories, feel its hollowed spirit.

"I live through them," came a soft voice behind me.

I jump, turning. There, at the doorway to the bedroom was a blond youth. He looks like one of those androgynous young gay prostitutes that you see occasionally near the Garden Park.

But there is something odd about him. Some ineffable quality. I tilt my head staring, trying to feel him, even at this distance.

"Juan?"

"I'm glad that you have come," he says.

"What are you? An Aztec or something?" I ask. I am amazed at how calm I feel. My hands are trembling.

"What?" he looks confused for a moment, and then recovers.

"Maybe I was, once," he tells me. "I don't remember. Only the skins remember, I don't. My past goes back only so far as they do."

"We've been doing it a long time," he continues.

We? Is he talking about the skins he wears? I don't think any of them agreed to any of this.

"I'm not sure, any more, how it started, or where I came from. I have books I've written that I can no longer read. The skins that had that knowledge are long gone. That's why I treasure the old ones."

He's just talking, as if we're friends.

"What?" I ask.

"I'm glad you followed the magic," he says. "That you came willingly. It makes it better."

"I'm leaving," I tell him, reaching into my purse for the mace. The obsidian knife presses itself into my hand instead, eager to be held. Fine, I give in. I show it to him, threatening.

"Don't try to stop me."

I brush past him, walking down the hallway and out into the living room. He comes padding after me, following at a respectful distance.

"Don't leave," he says, from the hallway.

The command stops me at the door, my hand on the knob. I desperately want to get out. To run. But I can't. Can't turn the knob. Can't open the door. Can't walk out and down the hallway out into the street and away.

I turn, watching him as he came out into the living room. The furnishings are twice as hollow now, twice as fake after what I've seen. The apartment is a lie, a cheap plastic mask concealing monstrosity.

"You don't feel hungry or thirsty. But you feel restless. As if something isn't quite there. You fidget, not comfortable with yourself," he tells me knowingly, his voice almost melodic.

"Leave me alone," I say desperately, I feel like a little girl, weak and helpless. All hollow stomach and trembling knees.

"You came here," his voice whispers softly.

"I'm leaving."

"You came here," he tells me. "Don't you want to know why? It's because you were called. Because my magic binds your skin, like all the others."

"No," I say.

"And do you know what that smell is?" he asks, slyly.

He pauses, and I see him grin. I look into his eyes and see a horrid delicious enjoyment.

"That smell is your flesh rotting, underneath your skin."

"I'm dead?" I ask abruptly, not quite shocked.

He shrugs eloquently.

"Sort of."

He's enjoying it.

I start to tremble.

"It's all right," he tells me, "you'll get used to it. I'll take care of everything."

He steps towards me.

I back up.

"It's all right," he soothes. He takes another step. "Give me the knife."

"I want to know something," I whisper.

"What is that, Chiquita?" he asks. "What is it that you wish to know? There'll be no secrets between us; we'll be closer than lovers."

I back up a step, and he advances again. His brown calm eyes looked into mine.

"Give me the knife," he sings softly, "you cannot resist."

But I can I realize as strength drains out of me. I can resist. I can feel the heat of the amulet, giving me strength, giving me a measure of free will. It isn't much, but it is there.

"Why me?" I whimper, my hands trembling as they grip the knife.

He stop, perhaps surprised that I have strength to ask. He gives me a half smile, his soft brown eyes twinkling, and then shrugs eloquently.

It was the shrug that said it. That does it for me. Something snaps.

"Bastard," I scream. The twenty nine dollar amulet is searing hot between my breasts. The knife flashes.

He stares at the hilt in his chest. Dumbfounded.

I want to vomit, my guts heave. Rage builds up in me, coursing through like she was a river.

"You Bastard," I scream, grabbing him by the shoulders and wrenching him around. He's surprisingly light under my hands. "Why? Why me? What did I ever do to you? To anyone?"

Tears are rolling down my face.

"Why me?" I scream at it as it struggles on the floor. I reach down, gathering the skin of its neck in my hands. It gathers easily, loose and squishy between my fingers.

"I had a life," I yell at him. "I was going to have dinner with Claire. We were going to go shopping. I had an appointment with my dentist."

"I had credit cards. I had an apartment!" I pull.

With a wet sucking noise, the skin begins to come loose from it.

"I had friends, and family, and a job. I had a whole life," I scream, red faced, trembling with rage. "It might not have been terrific, but it was mine. It was as good as anyone's."

The skin comes free. Juan collapses away, and suddenly I'm holding the skin of a pretty boy, for a moment, there's a memory of turning tricks in a parked car behind the Garden. It's not my memory. I fling the skin away.

The thing underneath it, that was wearing it, Juan, rolls there on the carpet, slickly wet and mewling.

I'd expected it to be red underneath, but it wasn't. Its slimy, almost translucent really. I can see through the skin, the musculature is just grey. I can see shadows in its abdomen. Its heart, lungs, liver and intestines. There's soft motion as its organs heave wetly against each other.

It is small and slender, almost childlike, and it has no genitals at all.

Of course not, those came with the skins.

"How dare you!" I kick it. "How could you take all that away from me? How dare you just come in and stop my life!"

"I was going to do things. Have kids. Get married. Get old. I was going to travel."

I kick it again. It tries to crawl away, mewling. The knife slips from its chest and it reaches for the hilt.

"Oh no," I told it, "No you don't!" Grabbing the knife away, I bend down and seize its wrist. Its flesh is cold and slimy; it's like holding oysters in my hand. I squeeze, deforming soft bones. It writhes, it's free hand flapping against me ineffectually. It pulls at my skin, and I feel some of the black X's of electrical tape come loose. I know what it wants, I won't let it. I slash at it with the knife, and it's skin opens, viscous oil seeps out of the wound.

"Not so tough now?" I ask it bitterly. "All your power is in the skin, isn't it? Without someone else to wear, someone else's life to suck, you're nothing."

Holding the wrist, I saw into the hand with the knife. Its eyes roll. You better be scared asshole, I think. It squeals.

"Who gave you the right?" I ask it.

I slam its head against the floor. I dig my fingers into its arm as it feebly tries to defend itself.

"Who gave you the right to do this thing to me?"

The fibrous muscles of its arm part as my fingers sink in. I take a good handful and yank.

"Where does it say that you can just walk up to a complete stranger and take everything away from them? I never even saw you before."

"It was my life, how dare you make it an accessory for your wardrobe."

It's whole body convulses as a chunk of muscle tissue rips loose, flopping wetly around my hand like a rotting steak.

I'm straddling it now, almost beyond words. I'm enraged by the injustice of it all. The sheer pointless awful knowledge of what's been done to me. Thirty seconds here. Ten seconds there. If my life had just been a tiny bit different, turned a different corner, stopped when I was moving, or moved instead of pausing, he'd have missed me. It was just a stupid fluke. Ten seconds and everything would have gone on and I'd have the rest of my life.

I dig my fingers into the chest, translucent gray muscle tissues parting as before. I feel the curves of ribs and hook my fingers, pulling.

It's body comes part way up with me. Struggling with its good hand, trying to push me away.

I pull again. There is an audible sound of bones cracking. Then suddenly it gives way, and I fall off it. Masses of ribs and tissue are clutched in my hands. It's soft and slimy, the bones feel like rubber.

I flung it away.

The translucent gray body convulses three times, and then lies trembling.

My skin's slid off my shoulder. I can feel it hanging there. I can feel one breast sliding down. Absent mindedly I tug it back into place. The gore stains my blouse. Some distant rational part of my mind notes this. It's a silk blouse, very expensive; I remember buying it, being thrilled with it.

I don't care.

I climb to my knees, staring at it.

Something is happening to it.

Suddenly, something wet and viscous and shapeless rears out of the chest cavity, before flopping back.

"Shit!" I say.

It pulls again. The skinless body seems to collapse in on itself, becoming hollow, and shrunken, as whatever is inside heaves.

It comes flowing out. A gigantic slug; flattening against the carpet. Its base ripples as it squirms, its head lifting, thick stalks, like feelers or antenna, waving back and forth.

"Hey Juan," I whisper softly, backing up against the wall. My legs bumps a bookcase behind me. I reach back, not taking my eyes off it. My left hand rests against the spine of a John Updike hardcover.

"Is it really you?" I ask. "Is this what it comes down to?" I slide the book from its shelf. It is hard and heavy in my slick hand.

Its feelers wave in the air. It's blind and slow and helpless.

"A slug?"

I hurl the book.

"A fucking slug," I shout, the anger coming back.

Abruptly the rage is back full force and I find herself screaming incoherently as I hurl book after book until the shelf was empty.

It flops and curls around itself in panic, its stalks withdrawing almost all the way into its body. As its sides lift, I can see hundreds of little squirming tentacles under it.

"That's it? Just a slug? Nothing but a slug?" I yell at it. I fling magazines at it, and then a coffee mug, and finally the coffee table. It bounces off.

"I'm really disappointed." It was almost funny. It's a joke. I start to laugh.

I stop myself abruptly.

The thing isn't really hurt, just confused.

I want to hurt it. To pay it back for the terrible thing it has done to me. To make it suffer.

I don't want to touch it.

I had a sudden image of it sliding into me, displacing my corpse, filling out my empty skin. Of being nothing more than a hollow puppet, saying the words, doing the things it wants.

The kitchen, I thinkt abruptly. There should be something in the kitchen.

"I'll be right back, Juan," I call, cheerfully.

There is a vertiginous moment of unreality. I sound so normal in my ears, for a second I'm not sure it's my voice at all, but rather a hallucination or some sitcom from television cutting in.

I step into the kitchen and pulled the cutlery drawer out.. Running my hands through the contents and I let them fall to the floor.

Who cares if somebody steps on knives? I was dead and Juan is a slug.

I heft butcher knives, considering one then another.

Not enough.

What I want is a fireman's axe. Something good and heavy. Something with a pleasing chop.

I look around.

There's the blender. Looks heavy.

Quickly, I grab it. It must weigh ten or fifteen pounds. With a yank I pull the power cord from the electrical outlet. I tossed away the blender cup, leaving a satisfying hunk of metal dangling from a heavy cord.

"Juan?" I call sweetly.

I step into the living room.

The slug was gone. There's only the skin, laying there in the corner, and the hollowed out wreckage of the body.

There's a trail of slime.

"Juan?" I called.

The trail leads down the hallway, towards the bedroom.

"There you are," I say, from the doorway of the bedroom.

It's struggling to reach the closet. It's wealth of skins. It can't move very fast.

What was it trying to do, I wondered? What did it want? Could it use the skins to fix itself? Regain its power? Slip into someone more comfortable, a big strong tough guy? Or maybe a wolf or a bear?

I don't intend to let it.

"I have something for you, Juan," I tell it. Wrapping the end of the power cord around my right hand, I tighten it, and then swing the blender around in a stiff arc, smashing it into the slug.

It screams satisfyingly then, an almost human wailing sound. The blender catches it in its middle, tearing its leathery hide. Slug gore splashes. Yellow mucus, with tubes and tubules writhing inside spill out.

It arches, and on the underside of its head, surrounded by a forest of waving feelers, I see its mouth. Or at least, the part that makes the wailing sound.

I pull the blender out of its body; it comes with a wet sucking noise, and swing it again, like a mace, smashing the pulpy form.

I do it again and again until the slug hide is torn to pieces; until specks of slime spacklee me; until the walls and the floor is covered with pieces of gore and writhing tubules.

"Just a moment, Juan," I tell it. "I'll be right back."

I dart off to the kitchen and return momentarily with plastic bottles.

"Lysol," I announce brightly, splashing it around. Wherever it touched pieces of the slug it hissed and sent up an acrid smoke.

I make sure to get every bit of Juan. Even the pieces that try to get away.

&&&

Back in t e living room, I gingerly press my foot against the face of the husk body. It gives slightly. I apply more pressure until it collapses entirely, like some badly made clay bowl.

I stare at the skin that used to be a blonde boy. I don't want to touch it any more, remembering the flash of memory. It was alive, like the others. Like me.

I sit heavily in the chair.

What am I going to do now? I wonder.

My life, I realize now, is over. I had tried to deny it, to pretend. But, I had understood that perfectly in the confrontation with Juan.

I was dead. My body is rotting under my skin. It would slowly fall to pieces. I csn smell my body decaying.

What now? Follow in Juan's footsteps. Preserve my existence by stealing bodies.

No. That won't work. I'm not a creature like Juan; I'd just been a victim, an overcoat. It wouldn't work the other way around. People wear overcoats, but overcoats don't go around looking for people to wear them.

The apartment reeks of Lysol and the sweet smell of Juan's corpse. Corpses, I correct myself. I'm a corpse too. All those skins, half alive. That shell, and the ruined body of the slug. The plac is full of dead things.

My life is over, I think sadly. I feel a vast and poignant sadness. So much is gone, so much is lost. And for what? Nothing.

Days ago, I'd been alive.

Now I'm dead.

My skin is alive, and here I am trapped in it, while my body rots.

I thought about going somewhere. Doing something. Answering my phone messages or having a fling or putting my affairs in order, while I still could.

"I want my life back," I whisper to no one in particular. Nobody hears me but the skins, who agree, but can do nothing.

It wasn't going to happen. It didn't matter.

It was all meaningless.

I sit there.

It grows dark in the apartment.
I don't care..
The phone begins to ring.
I look at it.

The End

Killing Hot

"Hot," the old man cackled, as he stepped up to the gas pump. "Killing hot."

"I suppose so," Gerry replied as he eased himself from the seat of the pickup truck. "Kind of humid."

It was a blistering hot day and his shirt was drenched with sweat. As he moved, it clung for a moment to the vinyl covering of the truck seat, before letting go and plopping wetly against his skin. He didn't much like it.

His greasy black hair was plastered in limp strips to his forehead. He squinted critically into the door mirror. He should be hard and lean like Clint Eastwood. Like a man on a terrible mission.

"Fillerup?" the old man said.

Gerry looked back at the codger.

"Fill her up?" the old man said patiently, holding the nozzle of the gas pump. He held it at waist level; it leaned forward like some flaccid metal erection.

Gerry bit his lip in disgust and nodded 'OK.'

The old fart probably diddled kids in his spare time. You couldn't trust anyone; that was the problem with the world today. His sister had discovered that.

Carefully, Gerry picked his white cowboy hat up off the passenger seat. Only fools wore hats while driving, his daddy used to say. He wiped his brow with a kerchief before setting it on his head at a jaunty angle.

He looked around.

There was a small convenience store attached to the gas bar. He strolled inside, maintaining his cool.

Gerry casually examined the bulletin board, looking for notices. Someone was trying to sell a pickup truck. Someone else had kittens to give away. No missing persons.

He checked the freezer section, looking for children's faces on milk cartons. There were two different brands represented, he identified four faces, one he hadn't seen before.

According to the information on the Cherry Flavoured Milk Carton, a blond haired blue eyed eight year old boy named Tommy Simkin had vanished about seven months ago. Interesting.

His sister had been blond and blue eyed. She'd vanished when she was twelve.

Gerry hated cherry flavoured milk. Milk should taste like milk, he felt, not candy. He bought a carton anyway, along with an assortment of chocolate bars and potato chips. There was a local weekly paper. He bought that too. And a regional daily newspaper. He picked that up as well.

The old woman at the counter looked disapprovingly at the mess he dumped in front of her. After she rang it up, Gerry paid for his purchases, pulled crumpled bills from his pocket.

"That stuff ain't good for you," the old woman told him, after he'd bought it.

The old man came in, he paid for the gas.

He took another look at the old man, closer this time, and let him go. The old fart, whoever he was, was probably all right.

Gerry walked back to the truck, blinking in the harsh sunlight as he took his cowboy hat off. He placed it carefully on the passenger seat.

It was here, all right, he thought as he started up the truck. He could feel it. He'd read the signs from a distance, and now that he was here, he could almost smell it. Killers, Child molesters, rapists, just plain evil, it left a residue, if you knew how to look for it.

Gerry knew how to look for it. And he knew what to do
when he found it. His eyes found the mirror, and he squinted
harshly, just like Clint Eastwood.

He drove into town.

&&&

The first thing that Gerry did after he got into town and
rented a room at a boarding house, was to take the cherry
milk into the bathroom. After carefully pouring its contents
down the sink, he cut out the picture of the boy with a
switchblade, and washed away the film of milk that remained.

The second thing he did was go to the Library. Sometimes
it would be the town newspaper office. Once he'd served as
an orderly in a small town nursing home, listening to the
stories the old men and women told each other. Other times,
he'd posed as a journalist doing a feature on rural life. Or as a
photographer for National Geographic. Or as an
anthropologist.

Generally though, he preferred to go to the libraries. It
was the best place to start. Gerry didn't feel all that confident
with people. He liked it best when he could meticulously
burrow through reams of paper; lose himself in the
accumulation of detail.

He found it kept him from thinking about his sister.

Newspapers were the easiest places. Gerry started with
the local weekly, slowly working his way backwards. He
flipped through the pages with practised efficiency, noting
births, deaths, ages, circumstances, community events,
disappearances. Looking for patterns.

Gerry had found that he was sensitive to patterns. He
could, with a little investigation, identify the subtle traces of
rapists and Satanists, feel the invisible webs of serial killers
and child molesters.

Once in a while he made notes in a little notebook he kept
with him. Occasionally, he would take a newspaper over to
the photocopier to retain some article.

He'd wondered sometimes why other people didn't notice
these patterns. But then, people were too wrapped up in their
lives to see what was in front of them. That was why it took a

stranger to see what they couldn't. A stranger who knew what to look for.

It was a strange and terrible thing to have a mission, an unending quest. He felt chosen by fate and wished that it had passed him by, that someone else had been chosen.

Ever since the awful thing that had happened to his sister, Gerry knew what to look for.

He finished with the local paper; it had only gone back two years. He'd have to go down to the newspaper office after all. Tomorrow.

Gerry began going through the regional newspapers, sifting through vague hints and alluring clues. Some notes he made for future reference, the traces of other monsters in other places.

A gang of children ran squealing through the library, the Librarian chasing after them. Gerry looked up startled. There was a tinkle of laughter that reminded him of his sister. He stared at the children, fascinated, until simple caution made him return his gaze back to the newspapers. Still, his heart thudded in his chest and his palms went clammy.

&&&

Alone in his room that night, fat body soaking with sweat, he masturbated roughly, staring blankly at the ceiling. When he was done he went and sat on the toilet and wept.

Afterwards he scrubbed himself ferociously in the shower, almost clawing at his smooth flabby flesh, gasping under the scalding water.

Gerry laid awake the rest of the night, thinking of his sister.

&&&

Sometimes it took a while to find them. A slow sifting of bulletin board notices and newspaper clips, poring through high school yearbooks, of carefully eavesdropping on town gossip.

This time, Gerry was driving by the park, when he saw him. Parks were a favourite haunt of them. It was where they found their victims, or did their deeds.

It was a fat greasy kid with lank black hair and sweat stains. There was something in the way he moved, not the usual random jerkiness, but a controlled malevolence that spoke of secrets and cruel cowardly violence. His eyes, when he looked up at Gerry's truck passing, squinted.

Gerry knew.

It was part of the gift, sometimes, to spot them so easily. Some adjunct to his mission. He'd never missed, never made a mistake. Sometimes Jerry wondered if there wasn't something supernatural behind it all.

He drove quickly around the block. As he returned, he could see the fat kid was still there.

A blinding image swept through his mind of what the fat kid had done to his victims. Sweating thighs heaving against screaming child body, blond curly hair wrapped in brutal hands. With an effort, he pushed it out of his mind.

A good distance off, he parked and waited. When the fat boy finally left, he followed from a discrete distance.

The boy walked slowly, but eventually, they came to an area that seemed devoid of witnesses. Gerry decided it was time to make his move. As he drove up, he carefully picked the white cowboy hat off the passenger seat and set it on his head. Mournful strains from a Clint Eastwood western filtered through his mind.

He idled beside the kid, not quite stopping, because the boy, after a single hostile glance, had kept walking.

"Want a ride?" Gerry asked, smiling.

The boy looked up. Gerry could see black piggy eyes.

"I'm all right," the boy said.

Fine. Do it the hard way. He stopped the truck.

Gerry showed him the nine millimetre pistol.

"Get in," he said as the kid abruptly stopped and turned pale.

Almost trembling, the boy walked stiffly to the passenger side of the truck and pulled himself in.

Gerry stared at him for a moment with naked disgust. Then he began driving, the truck lurched forward.

The town gave way to countryside. Woods and cottages proliferated, and gave way themselves to shacks and farmhouses marking their presence by battered tin mailboxes beside the road. Pavement shifted to dirt road, farmers' fields stretched in every direction. Heat shimmer rose from the road and the sun glare bounced off the hood of the truck.

"Killing heat," Gerry thought.

After half an hour the fat pig in the seat next to him gathered up enough courage to play innocent.

"Where are we going?" he asked.

Gerry shrugged.

"What's this about?" he asked, a few minutes later. "I didn't do anything."

Denial of course. Before they're even accused, they would start denying. It was one of the signs.

Gerry did his Clint Eastwood squint, never taking his eyes off the road. With one hand, he jammed the gun up against the bloated, sweating flesh of the boy's neck. The boy gasped and his eyes rolled in fear. He began to blubber.

Gerry shot him a sidelong glance thick with contempt. They kept driving.

Finally, they found a place, distant enough and isolated enough. Gerry drove into a farmer's field. He stopped.

"Get out," he told the kid.

He waited for the boy to get out, then he reached over and shut and locked the passenger door. The seat was slick with the boy's sweat. Again, Gerry felt a twinge of disgust.

Gerry got out and walked around the truck, until he was a few feet from the boy. They faced each other, flaccid, dumpy mirrors of flesh, perspiring in the afternoon heat. But Gerry wore the white hat, and he had the gun.

He waved; they walked away from the truck.

Thirty feet off, Gerry called a halt. It was time for the moment of truth.

"You did it," Gerry said flatly.

"What?" the boy said, faking confusion. "What did I do?"

"You did it to her," Gerry said. Blond hair and curls flashed through his mind. A terrible terrible thing.

"Who?" the boy said, trembling. "Who are you talking about? Who did I do? What am I supposed to have done?"

The boy was in the middle of "...I didn't do anything.." when Gerry, abruptly tired, slammed a bullet between his feet.

The boy yelped, and would have run, but Gerry had the sights right at his forehead. The boy turned paler than he was already.

"No more lies," Gerry told him, his Clint Eastwood voice squeaking. "The truth or I'll shoot you where you stand."

"But I'm telling the truth," sobbing.

"I'll shoot you."

"What do you want?"

"Say you did it."

"Did what?"

Another shot between the feet. Another yelping cry. The kid's bladder released, urine staining a wide path down his jeans. Gerry restrained an urge to shoot him out of simple disgust.

Look at him, he thought, fat and sweating and stinking of fear and piss, a mind like a sewer full of slime and puke. Shoot him now; I'd be doing him a favour.

"All right! All right!" the boy screamed. "I did it, whatever it was, I did it. Okay. Whatever it was, I'm sorry."

Finally. A palpable relief coursed through Gerry. The sweet satisfaction of their confessions. Sometimes, he didn't think he could live with himself without their confessions.

"You did it to her?"

"Who?"

The gun raised menacingly.

"I don't know who," the boy wailed, "tell me."

"You remember, a little girl, blond hair, curls."

"No! Yes! Oh God, don't shoot me, please. All right, I did it. Is that what you wanted?"

Gerry listened to the boy whine and grovel for a few minutes. A formless mixture of denials and confessions, begging and pleading, self-pitying whining.

Gerry felt strong. He felt proud and right. This was his mission, what he was made for.

"How many others?" Gerry asked.

"That's all. Some. I don't know. Lots. For God's sake, what do you want!"

Gerry licked his lips.

"Tell me what you did to her." Gerry ordered. "Exactly. Everything."

He felt a stirring in his pants.

It was as if the boy sensed it too. He stopped abruptly, staring at Gerry with big eyes.

"Are you sick or something?" he said softly, forgetting himself.

Gerry shot him in the face. The boy pitched forward, dead. Gerry kept shooting him anyway. He walked right up to the boy, emptying the pistol into the limp form. Tears ran freely down his face, he barely noticed.

&&&

Gerry stared at his notebook. There were signs of another child molester in the next town. A satanic cult appeared to be operating in a nearby city. He couldn't deal with them right away though, not with a fresh corpse in the area.

He'd go up north. There were plenty of indications in his notebook. Plenty of evil to stamp out. Plenty of fat sweaty boys with squinting piggy eyes and slimy little minds.

He thought of his sister again, of how she looked afterwards. He had to punish them for her. Punish them all. That was his crusade.

Like an avenging angel, Gerry roamed from town to town along the back roads of America. Hunting the scum of the earth. He felt chosen for this mission, and sometimes he wished it was someone else who had been chosen.

Carefully, he put his white justice hat on the passenger seat. He'd put a sheet down first so the boy's presence wouldn't stain it. He filed another small notch in his pistol. He counted the notches. It made him feel strong.

Then, as strains of music from some forgotten western trickled through his mind, lank wet hair falling flat across his forehead, he drove out of the farmer's field, into the sunset.

The End

The Dead Quarter

The second sun had just passed its peak when Killeen saw them. Most living things that could, sought shelter when the second sun was overhead. But the dead were often uncaring of such things. Shambling, they advanced upon him, their burnt and rotting flesh no longer quite recognisable as human.

Ordinarily, the living and the dead left each other quite alone, lost in their respective tragedies. But some among the dead hungered. They sat, or lay insensate, until some passing prey stirred them to act out the memories of their lives.

Killeen clutched his bundle of papyrs and held his staff at ready. He counted some seven of them, all at about the same state of decay. They were all around him, closing in, he could not tell, from the rags which remained to them, what they had been in life. Some carried weapons suggestive of the river kingdom before the war.

He swung his staff, but it did no good. They were upon him. Disdaining weapons, ignoring his blows, they bore him down. Teeth bare of lips or gums snapped inches from his flesh, as he tried to push them away.

In desperation he screamed, "Grandfather, Grandfather, have you forgotten me!"

A slackening? He couldn't tell, there were so many and their clawing at him so relentless.

"Grandfather, would you devour your own!" Some dead feared nothing so much as the thought of destroying those who were remembrances of its life.

Painfully his head was bent back, exposing his neck. Then suddenly a weight was pulled from him. Gasping he saw the largest of the dead smashing at its companions. Twisting hard, he rolled away, tearing a mummified arm with him. He struggled to his feet and ran.

He ran until they were no more than specks in the distance. His lungs burned and his guts heaved uncontrollably, he fell to his knees and voided his stomach as he coughed. He considered the mess with regret; he had lost his provisions, and his staff. All he had left were the precious papyrs for the Astronomer. Although what use the Astronomer would make of it, he could not say, as the Astronomer had died some three years ago.

He felt a pressure on his thigh, and jumped. The torn arm still clutched at him. Gingerly he pried it loose, keeping a careful watch for the dead. They were still on the horizon, but he well knew that the Horizon was not as far as it had been in times past. They did not appear to be coming after him, but the dead were often protective of their remnants, and the owner of the limb would doubtless be drawn to it.

He judged it would be best to continue. It would be hard travelling, but as nearly as he could tell, he would reach the city at the end of the world by the second rising of the third sun.

The second sun was setting now, and while the first sun radiated gentle warmth upon the world, its light could not fill the sky. The stars came out. He counted them, as he had done a thousand times before. All seventeen of them. All the stars left in the sky after the gods had their war.

The land Killeen passed through still had not recovered from that war. Perhaps it never would. He followed a dried riverbed. Occasionally he came in sight of ruins, and always avoided them.

He was low on provisions, having saved little but the papyrs from the dead.

As he walked, he charted orbits within his mind. More through habit than interest, he turned over equations worn smooth by the endless operations of celestial mechanics.

The astronomer had once speculated that before the war, it was the world and every other celestial body that turned about the sun, rather than the other way around, and pointed to a number of anomalies to support this view.

Regardless, it was now clear to all that, whatever things may have been, these three new suns turned about what was left of the world.

Just before the second sun peaked again, if it could be called peaking, he came to a farm and took shelter with them. The farmer was a dour man, who sat staring at him while the second sun blazed above.

Overhead the sky crackled and belched as the second sun blazed and guttered and emitted great gouts of flame. Killeen had speculated that the second sun followed a highly elliptical orbit and at its perihelion passed through the upper atmosphere. Today the sun guttered and sputtered for an hour, nine years ago when the phenomena was first observed it had lasted some ten seconds. This suggested an eccentric orbit growing steadily more eccentric.

Killeen did not share his speculations as to where this might lead.

When the sun had finally passed, the farmer offered Killeen the use of his daughter, a thickly boned lass of bovine eyes. He declined. The farmer offered the use of, first his sons, then his cattle. Each time, he politely declined.

Instead, he paid the farmer from his copper coins for new provisions. The cow eyed girl provided him with a carrying sack, her fingers lingering on his hand. He was given vegetables he could not name, but was told they could be eaten, so long as one did not dwell overlong on their shapes. Some of these vegetables twisted in quite disturbing ways.

The sky rumbled, a storm was building. From this at least the dead would seek shelter. The rains waterlogged their desiccated tissues, bloating them so that the flesh became soft and puffy, sometimes even falling away. Killeen had seen fierce rains strip a dead down to the bones, leaving only a skeleton, to collapse grinning in dark surprise.

He made sure his papyrs were well covered and took his leave as the rain began to fall. He carefully skirted the ghost pole which served to trap wandering disembodied spirits, and was once again upon the road.

The first sun had finally set when the wagon came up behind him. It was drawn by two trolls in harness, and was a long covered rig. He paid the toll to one of the trolls and was permitted to climb aboard. Within the wagon were a couple of elves, a family of gnomes, a human like himself, and some dead. No one felt the need to speak, and they reached the city in silence.

As Killeen walked through the gate he could hear the distant roar of the edge of the world. This was the city at the end of the world, it was also the city of twenty-one kings, the city of the new pantheon of gods, and in fact, the last city left in all that was left of the world. It was a small place for so many titles. The great cities were now blasted ruins.

The Astronomer had come here three years ago. He had left the observatory forever, to gather here with the other wise men, at the last repository of learning. He had died on that long journey. At first no one realised, the Astronomer had never been overly particular about hygiene, but then they noticed the maggots.

All three suns were down, and the rains had ceased in the cool night. He wandered the streets until he found a rooming place in the Dwarves ghetto. Many of the races kept to themselves, forming islands within the city. But men, it was held, were as common as lice, and wandered everywhere. With the last of his coins he paid for his lodging and then slept for what could be called a night and a day.

When he arose, he ate the last of the vegetables, careful not to look at them, and consumed some lizard meat. Lizard had become popular for meat, as had any creature thought to be without soul.

Thus fortified, he spent the rest of the morning hunting vermin, slowly gathering roaches, beetles, worms, and even a small mouse. Each of which he carefully packed so that they would not injure each other. When he felt he had enough, he went to the gateway by the river.

He had no difficulty with the first Gatekeeper, who was human, and whose only task was to prevent anything from coming back across the river. He crossed the covered bridge without difficulty listening to the sudden hail of raindrops. Beneath him the water flowed slow and tepid, its surface continually dancing in the rain. Strange colours seeped through it.

The Gatekeeper on the other side of the bridge was dead, and had been dead a long time. It challenged him. He offered a small handful of vermin. No expression passed the withered mummified features.

After a long hesitation it took the offering. He walked past, careful not to look at what the guardian did with its new prize.

The dead quarter was dark and dry. The clouds that continually hovered over this section of the city rained only at the edges of the dead section.

The architecture of this part of the city had an odd feel to it. Shabby and antique, it seemed preserved; as if mimicking the mummified nature of its inhabitants.

There was no Heaven or Hell left, no Valhalla, no Limbo. The war of the Gods had destroyed the realms of good and evil, and the realms of afterlife. The dead, having no place else to go, returned to reanimate their bodies with decaying magics.

Eventually, like everyone else, they came here. To the last city, to wait in the dead quarter while the remnant of the world groaned on its axis.

He was frightened as he walked down the street, clutching his parcels. The memory of his previous encounter with the dead was fresh within him. He lit a torch, less for its light than his comfort. He passed a calcified giant standing in the middle of the road like a statue. He heard a slow grinding as it turned its head to look at him. Other dead turned in his direction, staring from vacant sockets. They sensed the glow of his life, and of the vermin he carried. One by one, they began to follow him.

By days at least, the living were safe in the dead quarter. Or relatively safe, he told himself. The periods when all three suns were gone from the sky were infrequent and brief.

The dead had their own economy, based on the trading of the tiny flares of insect's lives, with an occasional mouse or rat representing wealth. But they could and would trade with the living, offering useless gold for the nameless things they now desired. There was a particularly obscene appellation for the sort of living who came to trade with the dead. But the custom was established. He was safe.

For the moment.

Twice, the dead surrounded him. Both times he bought his way free with handfuls of beetles and earthworms. He did not look back.

Finally, he came to the black tower. There were nine towers in the city, each the home of some pathetic survivor of the war.

The self-styled new pantheon of gods.

The black tower stood in the centre of the dead quarter, it was a ramshackle affair, listing to the left, and looking as if some gigantic child had simply heaped one disparate building on top of another. It's' apex reached the clouds that shielded the quarter from the relentless suns; its base was a sprawling mass of black basalt. This was where the new God of Death held court.

The guards denied him entrance. They looked more human under his torchlight, more alive than most of the shambling rotting corpses that stood about. By signs they made him understand that the Lord of Death received the living only when the three suns were at their height.

It was getting very dark. He pushed past the dead who waited outside the tower. He had lost track of time here in the quarter where no sun shone. But as the perpetual twilight darkened he realised that all three suns must be setting. Whatever safety he had counted on would soon vanish.

He ran.

He ran through the streets as if devils were after him. Clutching his vermin pouch and the astronomer's papyrs in his hands, his feet rang across the pavement, as human and inhuman corpses turned towards him.

It was too late. The bridge was blocked by feral dead. They turned towards him in their varying stages of decomposition. He sensed their hunger. He turned and ran again. They began to spill from the doors and windows. He twisted and turned to avoid their clutching hands.

Suddenly, he found himself in an alley. Broken windows looked down on him in silent reproach. The hungry dead approached from both sides.

Suddenly a door opened not a dozen feet away from him. In the faint light of his torch stood a dead girl. For once death had been kind, her flesh was whole. Her lips had turned black, but her eyes remained, though in dark and sunken sockets, making her grimly alluring. The swollen firmness of decomposition lent her figure a beauty it had lacked in life, and the grey rags she wore barely hid it. Some of the dead, for no accountable reason, seemed not to rot at all. Above her breasts, over her heart, there was a wound. It was dry and bloodless, and to his sight it resembled a mouth with lips.

"Come," she said. Her voice was dry and whispering. It reminded him of autumn leaves spinning in the dust. He imagined he saw both sets of lips moving as she spoke again.

"Safe," she said.

That was enough for him. He followed her into the building. Together they passed through rooms and halls. They went up stairs, and down ladders, his possessions knocking around him. At some point he lost his torch, and knew himself to be completely in her power.

Finally, she led him to a room. Her room, he imagined, he could barely make out bits and pieces of the eccentric items the dead sometimes hoarded. The door was barred and bolted.

"Safe," she said, and he watched as both lips moved, and wasn't quite sure which had spoken. She began to undress.

Suddenly, he knew the price she wanted of him. The life she silently demanded.

"No," he whispered.

But the price was there, and eventually he paid it.

Afterwards, as he held her, warming her cold body and cold soul with his own, he felt a chill within him. He knew it would never go away.

The darkness passed, and with it, some of the relentless hunger of the dead. It was safe again, or at least, relatively safe. Together, they made their way back to the basalt gateway of the tower. Using the remainder of the slugs and worms he purchased an audience and was ushered into the chamber of the Dark Lord.

"Do you have an offering," the Dark Lord spoke for itself, from atop a black marbled throne. It was tall and pale with long spidery hands and burning red eyes. Two sharp fangs glinted from his mouth, for this was the last Vampire.

It was also maimed, missing three fingers from his left hand, its left eye was missing, and black scars covered the left side of its face. It had been a minor demon in the great battle, in surviving; it had inherited the threadbare mantle of divinity.

Carefully he reached into his vermin sack, and praying that it was still safe, offered the mouse.

The Vampire laughed. Its laughter went on and on, pealing down the silent halls where no bell would toll. The Vampire stood up and sat down, almost capered around its throne, alive with nervous energy contrasting the listlessness of its subjects.

Behind him, in an almost human gesture, the dead girl put her hand on his shoulder.

"A mouse," said the Lord of all Things Dead as it laughed. "I have sipped the blood of kings and queens, tasted demigods. Tell me, foolish mortal, what would you buy from me with a mouse?"

Killeen felt himself blush, conscious of the blood flowing just beneath his skin.

"I want the Astronomer. One of your subjects, come to this city inside these last three years."

"I know of the one you seek," said the Vampire. "The one who counted the stars as they went out. What do you want with that one?"

"I have his property," he could not think of the Astronomer as an 'it.' "I would return it."

Again the Vampire laughed.

"The dead have no property, give it to me and perhaps I'll forget about the mouse."

"I will give it to the Astronomer," Killeen refused.

The Vampire snarled and stepped down from its throne, approaching him. It's momentary humour giving way to snarls.

"Give it to me now, or I will take more than the mouse and you will rise three nights hence."

Killeen presented the cross, a religious symbol that had been the bane of such creatures. The Vampire stopped and regarded it. It laughed sadly.

"That God is dead," it told him, as it reached out and crushed the artifact. "And you would not rise after three days; you would just become another shambler."

They regarded each other. Killeen had nowhere left to go. He stood his ground. The Vampire loomed above him, and then suddenly, it seemed tired, as if it had been going through the motions.

"What is this property?" the Vampire asked finally.

"Papyrs. His notes and calculations. We charted the suns, they are slowly falling to earth," Killeen replied.

The Vampire laughed again. Softly.

"Then have the Astronomer," whispered the vampire, and gave the commands.

While they waited the last Lord of the Dead spoke. It spoke of how it was the last of its kind. Of how it had, after the final battles, walked into the sunlight to join its kin and burned to ashes, only to be reborn when night finally came. It spoke of weariness and despair. It no longer had a lust to end human lives; they all came to it sooner or later anyway. It and the others scraped together kingdoms from the fading remnants of creation, wending their way through a tired and empty existence.

Killeen felt the creatures despair; this was the true face of the creature, he thought, its rage and laughter but a cover for the emptiness it faced. It wormed its way into the chill in his soul. He fought it with his purpose.

Then the Astronomer arrived. He wore a brown monks robe and hood, but Killeen recognised the brisk and purposeful movements. Death had not dimmed the Astronomer. He stood before Killeen and pulled down his hood.

Death had played its joke. The Astronomers features were much as they had been in life, barely touched by its mortality. Except for the eyes. For there was nothing left but empty sockets. The maggots had been at work.

"You see what your struggles have come to," whispered the Vampire suddenly behind him, "This is what the world has become."

It was too much. Killeen snarled and hurled the bundle of papyrs at the Lord of Death. The bundle exploded and its sheets twisted in the air, fluttering to the ground like wounded birds.

"The world falls to pieces," he screamed, "and it's just a joke for you. You and your kind have power. Do something."

"We can't. Even together, we have not enough power left, to force a sun back up into the sky, and if we could, we would need still more power to keep from destroying it in the process," the Vampire replied sadly. "We cannot remake the world."

The dead girl reached out for Killeen, as if to save him from himself. But he went on.

"You `gods' sit bemoaning your lack of power. Creation was not made with power," he snarled. "It was made with art, and study. Intelligence, wisdom, skill was in the hand of the creators. Had you the courage to seek wit and wisdom, you might save what is left."

He forced the words out through his teeth.

The Vampire rose tall before them, and they fell back before its dark majesty. Killeen, the Astronomer, and the Dead Girl huddling together in the face of this thing that was both living and dead. A roaring filled the halls and the papyrs scattered flying. It gestured at the papyrs with the talons of its left hand. They flew together into a pile at his feet.

"Fool," said the Vampire, in an almost kindly way.

Between them the Astronomer gathered the papyrs in desiccated hands.

Killeen felt the dead girl pulling at him. He could not take his eyes off the creature.

He felt the Astronomer, turning the papyrs over, trying to unlock with the peculiar senses of death, secrets that it no longer had eyes for.

"Let's go from here," the Dead Girl urged. She would never speak so many words at once, again.

Cold winds howled through the chamber. The Astronomer held tight to the papyrs.

"You shall not leave this place." The Vampire said this half in anger, as if seeking a diversion from despair.

"Please," the dead girl's lips rasped in pleading.

The wind and the roaring faded as the Vampire bleakly considered them. Its dark countenance betrayed nothing.

The Vampire was silent for a long moment.

"Go," it said finally.

They fled, leaving the Astronomer behind, the dead girl lead him away.

Killeen in the end, found himself with no place to go.

He returned to the living parts of the city, but found no solace in the false gaiety of the living. There was no demand for his skills.

For a time, he worked as a scribe, studiously recording tallies of goods bought and sold for a local merchant. His employer was a taciturn man of substantial weight, scarred all down one side, as if he'd been caught by an unskilled butcher.

Killeen found the work undemanding to the point of futility, leavened only by his efforts to introduce higher mathematics to his bemused employer's books of account.

"We are all now," the Merchant told him once, as they sweltered beneath a roof, hiding from the conjunction of three kings.

"The Gods, the Demons, the Emperors and Kings. They made the world, and we simply lived in it. Now they are all gone, but we still live in the world they they made, or such ruins as are left. They say this world shall not endure. If so, it bears no thinking about, exist, proceed, embrace the pleasures of the flesh. There is no wine so sweet as the pleasure which flows from satin thighs."

During the very rare evenings, when the suns had passed beyond the horizons, and the clouds parted, he would go up to rooftops, and count the stars again and again, to make sure their numbers remained constant. Sixteen now. He judged that number was close enough.

Eventually, he grew bored with the Merchant, and for a time whiled away the hours as a manual labourer on public works half conceived and never completed, or temples systematically desecrated and deconstructed. The remaining Gods, or the reduced beings now called by that name, had little desire for worshippers, and preferred to remain cloistered in their towers. In any event, no one was inclined to worship them. So the state of disinterest was mutual and agreeable.

The orgies and revels held little interest for him, for he saw clearly the terror and despair that lay beneath the drunkenness and pursuit of pleasure. It was one such revel, that he learned from laughing girls that despite the Merchant's fondness for their wares, he no longer had the equipment to make use of them. His pursuits were merely for the sake of memory.

Only the Festival of Cursing the Gods held interest for him, and he joined with his fellow living in defiling the remaining effigies of those beings who had destroyed each other in their pride and arrogance, and doomed what remained of the world.

But even that was pretence he realized, hollow defiance. The true effigies and symbols had either been destroyed in the great war of the Gods, or smashed immediately after by the survivors. The effigies now being defiled were manufactured for that solitary purpose, each new generation of artifacts more elaborate in their built in flaws for maximally colourful destruction, each depiction of a God more humiliating and degenerate. The old Gods were gone, and the new ones past caring.

Out of frustration, he decided on a quest to visit each of the new Gods, to try and enlist them. The first three refused to see him, the priests denying his pleas and offerings.

The temple of the fourth was abandoned; he wandered the dusty corridors until he found what remained of the new God.

He visited no more temples after that.

Killeen found he wandered more and more frequently through the Dead Quarter, preferring their calm resignation. At first, he bought his passageway with the bright life-lights of insects and the occasional mouse, captured and caged for just such a purpose. But though such gifts were welcome, over time, they became unnecessary.

Instead, the Dead Girl would invariably appear, to become his guide and companion. She spoke little and he found her silence congenial. The price she demanded became more acceptable with each encounter. Often they would walk through the streets of the necropolis, her cold hand in his warm one.

Together they would commune with the blind Astronomer, and Killeen would while away the hours organising the venerable corpse's observations and calculations, left in a shameful state, not so much by death as the loss of sight.

Once, he looked up from his calculations, startled to find the Lord of Death solemnly watching his labours.

"So be it," the Lord of Death said finally. Killeen did not understand what that meant.

It would not have been a surprise to anyone who cared, if there had been such, when Killeen made the Dead Quarter his permanent residence, sharing quarters with the two beings he was closest to.

And yet, Killeen was restless.

The third sun went out finally, its blaze weaker than the others, its light fainter and farther away slowly died away entirely.

Ensconced in the Dead Quarter, he left it just as frequently to seek out the tales of refugees. The stories were always the same: The edges of the world crumbling away, rivers drying, cities dying. Far out in what passed for remote realms, desperate ghosts tied themselves to whatever might give them shelter, the dead walked and the living mourned.

Once, among the refugees, he met the farmer who had sheltered him, and the farmer's cow-eyed daughter, now both of them as deformed as the vegetables they had raised. He wondered what had brought them to this pass, had shaped and changed their bodies. But they did not know him, and he let them pass without speaking to them.

One mid-day the second sun blazed and burbled overhead, so that despite the clouds, everything was forced to take shelter, the God of Death found him in a basement, held him despite his struggles and drained him, dropping him.

For Killeen the passage of death was a surprise, numbness in some areas, a luminescent awareness in other ways. He had expected more, or perhaps less. How long had he lain dead? He was not sure. It seemed vaguely embarrassing to him, a species of laziness that his corpse should simply lay there as if it had no concerns at all.

He stood up. The Lord of Death had remained. Killeen brushed at his trousers. He had soiled himself in his death, something that seemed to embarrass the Vampire more than him.

The two found it difficult to look at each other. As if they'd shared some ill-considered act of passion and now regretted the impulse in their own ways.

After mumbling uncertainly, the Lord of Death departed, his final words: "It doesn't matter."

The experience left Killeen feeling awkward.

Death changed surprisingly little. He continued to keep company with the Astronomer and the Dead Girl. The Dead Girl's affections were unchanged by his new state. Perhaps she was so used to him it no longer mattered. Everything was as it had been. He continued his calculations and measurements.

He saw the Vampire now and then, so many of the Dead seemed to lack any kind of purpose. He supposed that even if the Vampire did not understand what they were doing, it still fascinated the creature. Sometimes he would look up from his calculations to see it watching him, as it had when he was living, and he would simply return to his work, ignoring it.

What more could it do?

The world, as broken as it was, simply rolled on, the stars in the sky, the ceaseless arcs of the sun, the common concerns of men and ants. The concerns of the living no longer weighed upon him, and he realized how little he'd cared for them in life. He wondered if, in some way, he'd been dead all along.

He did not miss breathing, or elimination, or the hundred little chores of the body, they had always seemed tedious, and he was glad to be without them. Sometimes he would stop for a moment and listen, then realize he was waiting for the sound of his absent heartbeat.

He never spoke of these things, though sometimes as he sat with the dead girl on the ledge of a building overlooking the city, their hands intertwined, he felt that perhaps she knew anyway.

The Vampire avoided them when the dead girl was with him. It could not meet her eyes.

The day came when the Dead burst from the Dead Quarter. The guards fled then, before the columns of the Dead. The living were hunted through the streets.

They fought as best they could, sorcerers cast their spells, soldiers fought and formed martial lines, guards built barricades, cowards fled, the fearful wailed, the clever hid, merchants offered money, prostitutes offered their bodies, and the hopeless begged.

It did not help any of them.

The living cursed the Lord of Death for his betrayal. They prayed and then cursed the gods for their absence.

Giant Monsters Sing Sad Songs / Page 95

It made no difference. Soldiers screamed battle cries as they were overwhelmed. Misers died with their hordes and mothers with their babies at their breasts. The dead spared no one. Only the hidden survived.

Undead fathers strangled their living children, enemies settled old scores, former lovers brought savage embrace. It did not matter; the whole city belonged to the dead now.

It made no difference.

The newly killed rose and raged, they wailed and smashed, a delegation protested to the Lord of Death. But eventually, they succumbed to apathy, to listless despair. And sometime after that, they returned one by one to their tasks and chores, having nothing better to do.

Killeen simply counted the stars. All fourteen of them.

The Astronomer ceased, already long dead and maggot eaten, he had slowly fallen apart, bit by bit, the fragments losing volition, until there was nothing left but a hungry ghost and scraps of personality clinging to remnants. But even these disintegrated, the personality worn through, the desiccated flesh withering, until even the ghost drifted away.

The air grew thin, though it hardly mattered to Killeen and the other dead. The erratic rains ceased altogether, which would have pleased the dead, had they the impulse to care. They no longer had to shield themselves from the rain bloat, only the scorching heat of the second sun, as it passed its' mid-day.

Time had come to mean little. Time had only ever served to mark events, and there was now little to mark that the dead cared about, only three events would bear notice.

The air grew so thin that the few living survivors, those who had managed to hide during the massacre, who had subsisted like rats in the new city of the dead, passed. They stumbled out into the streets, choking and begging for help, writhing in hours and days of agony, as the undead watched them.

These were the living who had fled the Lord of Death's gift, who had turned down his gentle mercy. The Dead respected their choice, had ignored their scuttling and hiding, had even abetted their scavenging. They had chosen to breathe to the last.

So the dead watched, but did not interfere, as each gasped and clawed the thinned air, their faces turning red and then black. Solemnly they watched the last of the living struggling for the last bit of poisoned air, watched their tongues protrude swollen, watched their eyes bulge and hearts stop.

Killeen understood that the purge of the living had been a mercy, rescuing so many from this fate. This was the fate that had awaited all the living, to lay choking and struggling in the dust.

The Lord of Death had been compassionate.

Some time after the last living person had died, Killeen entered the quarters of the Lord of Death.

For a time, he watched the Vampire's body hanging there, charting and measuring the small circular motions of the body's sway at the end of the rope.

There were no more gods at all, after that. But it didn't matter. The dead had no use for gods.

When the end came, it came without fear, without pain, without dread. The dead were beyond all these things.

Killeen's measurements and calculations were long complete, with the Astronomer's help; he had charted every pathway in the skies, and knew when and where they lead.

He took the dead girl up to the tallest building in the city. Together, they sat on the roof, facing southwest. He took her hand, which surprised them both, as it had always been her that reached out for him. For a passing instant, he felt a human impulse, to wonder at the needs that had driven her, even in undeath, to wonder at her name, or if she even remembered.

But then the flicker died. The dead had little use for empathy in their common solitude. He was surprised at the sentimentality left in him.

Above them, the second sun roared, guttering and sputtering as it descended towards the peaks in the distance. They held hands and watched as it finally crashed into the mountains.

They held hands, and Killeen turned to look at her one last time as the wall of flame rushed towards them.

The End

Regrets Child

The naked twelve year old blonde girl took three precise steps into the bedroom. She looked at the old woman lying unconscious on the bed, then she turned to Marietta.

"She's going to die soon," the girl said. She paused.

"I'm glad," she concluded.

Then she vanished.

For a moment the room was absolutely still. Marietta put her romance novel aside, got to her feet and walked to the place the girl had been. She shivered, the air had turned cold.

Marietta looked around. The room was empty. The house was empty and still. The only living things in the house were her and the old lady, Hattie, and a few plants that Marietta had brought to provide some color. Where had the child come from? And, more importantly, where had the child gone?

The girl had seemed to turn, as if about to step away, and had disappeared. It was like she'd stepped around a corner, or into a blind spot. Had she even been there?

No, Marietta decided, it was too vivid to be a hallucination.

One of the neighbours kids playing pranks, then?

The old woman was still sleeping.

Marietta searched the house, going from room to room, even inspecting the closets. In one room, she found an antique man's fob watch which she pocketed.

In the kitchen, sitting on the table, she found a twisted wire. She stared at it dumbly until she realized it was just a coat hanger that someone had unstrung. It was discolored, as if heated and cooled, like those hash knives addicts had. There was a faint acrid odor to it. Marietta swept it into the trash and checked the doors.

Locked.

Then she returned back to the bedroom, listening to the old woman's fitful breathing and reading her romance novel.

At the end of the shift she noticed that her plants had died.

&&&

On her way home, she thought she saw something out of the corner of her eye.

She turned. But there was nothing but the chill autumn wind blowing cascades of leaves down the barren street. The air felt gray and leaden, swollen with impending rain. Underneath the wet greyness there was the aftertaste of an odd sharp odor.

Marietta shook her head. What would a little girl be doing out on the street, naked, in weather like this?

&&&

"Nurse, what are you reading?" the Hattie asked. She wasn't that old, actually, only in her fifties. Barely twenty years older than Marietta herself. But cancer had a way of making things ancient.

Marietta jumped at the sound of her voice.

Terminal patients didn't talk much. There wasn't much to say that compared with the fact of their death. They didn't care about your likes or dislikes, your relatives and family, your plans or your future, and they had no future of their own. That didn't leave much to discuss.

Wordlessly Marietta showed her the book.

It was called "True Experiences With Ghosts," by Rhetta Schreiber.

Marietta watched the woman's lips move as she read the title.

Finally, the old woman sank back into the bed, breathing shallowly.

Giant Monsters Sing Sad Songs / Page 100

"Would you like me to turn on the television set?" Marietta asked. The television had been raised up onto a table at the end of the room, so that she could watch it more easily.

A lot of terminal patients did that, watched television or listened to the radio. Some of them played slow games of solitaire, or waited patiently for infrequent and excruciating visits from their relatives.

"No."

"The radio?"

"No."

"All right."

There was a long pause. Marietta watched the dust filter through the afternoon sunbeams as they crawled across the room.

This was her job, to go to people's houses and sit patiently while they died. Seeing to the occasional minor comfort or inconvenience, administering medicine.

"Nurse?"

Marietta put the book down again. The old lady was looking at her.

"Yes?"

"Do you have children?"

"No."

Thirty five and counting, her biological clock was ticking and there were few prospects in sight. Fewer each year. Sometimes she fantasized about picking up a random stranger, just for the occasion, and raising a baby on her own.

"How about you?" Marietta asked.

Generally, she tried to avoid personal involvement with her clients. It wasn't professional, and wasn't going to lead anywhere. There was no sense getting mixed up in things.

But she knew there were no visitors, and when the old woman had been sleeping, Marietta had leafed through the photo album. No birth notices, no baby pictures. The album had been as lifeless and antiseptic as the rest of the house.

It wasn't just the cancer that made Hattie look ancient, Marietta had realized. Hattie had aged quickly in those photographs. Some people did.

The old woman cleared her throat and licked her lips. Marietta reached for the squeeze bottle, but the woman waved her away. It had become cold in the room, Marietta reached over to adjust the woman's blankets.

"Ever been knocked up?"

"Excuse me," Marietta said, shocked.

The old woman's eyes glistened.

"I bet you liked it. Women like a man to go inside, but he leaves things behind and sometimes they grow."

"I really don't like this conversation," Marietta said.

"You got rid of yours didn't you?" the old woman asked, "Probably in a hospital with doctors and everything?"

"That's none of your business," Marietta said firmly.

The old woman just laughed, as if Marietta had said yes.

"I did mine the old fashioned way," Hattie laughed, "but I couldn't get rid of it."

&&&

Marietta poured herself a cup of coffee, and then, wearing her terrycloth bathrobe, wandered around her apartment examining her plants. She thought of the dead ones at Hattie's place.

Several weren't doing very well, she noticed. It was like that, sometimes in autumn. She watered and turned them, trying to position them for the best light in the morning.

It was a comfortable, if stark apartment. Somewhat like her life, she reflected.

Marietta turned on the television and flicked through stations. There was nothing on.

She tried to go back to her romance novel, but she had trouble concentrating.

When she finally put it down and picked up her coffee, it was cold at her lips, as if all the heat had been sucked out of it.

&&&

Marietta dreamed that she was sitting cross legged in her kitchen with the little girl. The child was casual about her nudity, sitting with legs splayed, but Marietta was cold and wore her bathrobe. There was a faint smell in the room.

They were cutting up pieces of paper with scissors.

"Did you love him?" the little girl asked. She was cutting out paper dolls. Boy dolls and girl dolls, big ones and little ones in elaborate chains. She passed them to Marietta, who would cut them apart.

Marietta shrugged.

"I was twenty-three. I thought I did. I guess I was just infatuated."

"You got pregnant," the girl's tone was accusing.

Marietta looked up from cutting a little doll in half.

"Snip, snip, up between the legs. Half dolls half lives," ran quietly through her mind, scampering on soft mouse feet.

"A woman doesn't need love to get pregnant," Marietta told her, "just sperm."

"You need love to keep it," the child said. For a moment, she looked just like Hattie, ancient and withered inside the little girl shell. The odor was stronger for moment.

"It wasn't a matter of love," Marietta said.

"It wasn't enough," the girl whispered, she'd dropped the scissors and was twisting the paper dolls in her hand, stretching them out. The paper became copper, almost metallic as it stretched like toffee into thin lines.

Marietta woke sweating. She looked at the digital clock beside her bed, it was 3:57. The room was ice cold.

She got up and made herself some coffee. She sat at the kitchen table, drinking cups of coffee, one after the other, as the dawn broke.

She was absolutely certain that if she went back to sleep she'd have the dream again. She didn't want to see what the little girl was making with her hands.

&&&

"Her medical file said she had some complications from a provoked miscarriage, I've never heard that term before."

Marietta sat in the elderly Doctor's private office. It wasn't an examining room, but rather a reading study. There was an oak desk, and distinguished volumes lining the shelves

It was a warm room. Marietta appreciated the warmth. It seemed that now every place she went was just cold enough to be uncomfortable.

"That's a very unusual question, Ms..." the Doctor's kindly eyes squinted, as if he was trying to recollect her last name.

"Marietta," she offered.

He nodded. "That's a very odd question, Marietta. I realize that you're Hattie's nurse, and highly recommended for the job...but I wonder at the relevance?"

Marietta wrung her hands, staring at her fingernails for a second. She was very tired. She'd been tired a lot, lately.

"Hattie likes to talk...about certain things, and I'm not sure how to respond."

The Doctor nodded.

"And you feel that discussing things here might allow you to deal with Hattie a little better?"

Marietta nodded.

The Doctor allowed a slow moment to drag out and twist in the air like a curl of cigarette smoke.

"I believe that you are a victim of fashion," he said at last. "There is nothing mysterious about the file, except for certain turns of phrase we used back then to try and make the bitter palatable."

Upon seeing the confusion on Marietta's face, the Doctor explained, "women were, in Victorian times, thought to be fragile creatures. Anything, a sudden shock, an exertion might provoke a miscarriage. Hence the origin of a delicate term."

"Women," he laughed softly, "are of course, far from fragile. The term came to be used in cases where provocation was extreme, and likely to invoke, under its own name, the unwanted law."

"It was an abortion," Marietta said.

The Doctor winced. "It was different in the old days. Miserable and desperate. It was against the law, so women would go to butchers or midwives or mutilate themselves. Then we'd be left with the mess, to try and salvage a life. We had whole hospital wards devoted to the leavings of botched abortions. These poor women had gone through enough without bringing the law into it."

"So you called it by another name," Marietta said softly.

The Doctor nodded.

"The complications?" Marietta asked.

"There were always complications," the Doctor told her. "The procedures were barbaric, without anaesthesia or sanitation. A lot of women bled to death, or died from toxic infections. Many who survived were sterile or mutilated, like Hattie. Some didn't quite succeed, and gave birth to babies, crippled or deformed in the womb."

"Hattie was mutilated?"

"She's talking about that now?" The Doctor looked up. He didn't wait for an answer.

"Hattie was one of the do-it-yourself girls. Probably safer than a back alley butcher. Do you know how she did it?" the Doctor asked.

The Doctor waited a silent beat.

"She used a wire coathanger. The traditional instrument. Her little innovation was to heat it white hot over an open flame."

"My God!"

"It should have killed her. Certainly, it did the job for the child, and for any other child she might have had.

"It started a fad actually; several other women tried the same thing. They all died."

He smiled ruefully, "sometimes I think of all those desperate frightened women, knowing or guessing the risks, but going ahead. I can't believe the right to lifers would drag us back to that. It really was horrible."

"I try not to think about it," Marietta said, "I try really hard."

"I don't think it was ever a decision that was made lightly," the Doctor said softly, "not then, not now. It's the kind of thing that leaves scars, on the body and on the soul."

On a moment of inspiration she asked, "Do you believe in ghosts."

He laughed softly.

"Only in a metaphorical sense."

She smiled. "What is a ghost? Metaphorically?"

"Ghosts are the things we've lost but can't let go," he paused to contemplate it.

"It is, perhaps, a terrible thing to be tormented by chances lost and possibilities unfilled or by children never had."

&&&

"What did you call it," Hattie asked from her bed.

Marietta looked up at Hattie, questioningly.

"I don't know what you mean," she said carefully.

That afternoon, when Marietta had arrived, late for her shift, she'd found the front entrance littered with paper dolls.

She supposed that neighborhood kids might have made a game of stuffing them through the mail slot. Though she had no idea why they would do such a thing?

Hattie smiled.

"That's good," she said, "You should never give them names. It gives them something to hold on to. A name changes things."

"Is that why," Marietta tried to ask, "Why...she stayed?"

Hattie shrugged.

"She was hard to get rid of, harder than most anything. She wanted to be born, that one. I tried just about everything. Potions, Doctors, before I had to do it myself."

She drifted off, lost in memories. Marietta waited patiently for a few minutes.

Out in the living room, a rhythmic squeak began. As if someone was sitting in a chair, rocking.

Marietta turned on the television set. She left the volume on low. Just loud enough to drown out the sound of the rocker.

"How can something rightly die if it wasn't rightly born?" Hattie mumbled as Marietta watched the price is right, "and where can it go?"

&&&

"Why are you so big?" Marietta asked the nude girl in her dream. She knew she was dreaming.

Once again, they were sitting in her living room, playing cards. It was a strange deck, almost like Tarot. Marietta in her dream state knew what all the cards were. She selected the Kindly Man, showing the figure of an elderly man weeping, face carefully turned away, hands in pockets. Marietta laid it face up on the pile.

The little girl studied the card for a moment, unselfconsciously scratching her genitals. Finally, she covered it with the twins.

The crude inks depicted Romulus and Remus as swaddling babes, drinking blood that streamed down the sides of an eviscerated she-wolf hanging from a hook. Its nipples dangled uselessly on either side of the gaping wound.

It was very cold in the dream, Marietta realized. Ice cold. Grave cold. Hungry cold.

The girl stared at the cards with satisfaction.

"She feeds me," the little girl said. "It's like this place in her that opened up and can't close, I drink from it. I suck life."

Marietta had a sudden image of the child bloating slowly like a tick, fastened to the body of her mother. The mother had Marietta's face. Hattie, she thought to herself, willing the face to change.

"You're killing her," Marietta said, and she knew it was true. She looked at her cards. It wasn't a very good hand. She played the drowning man, rope around his ankles, screaming for breath as something terrible dragged him down. "She's going to die."

"I know," the girl grinned.

"Die, dying, dead, dead dead," she chanted.

Marietta was suddenly conscious that she was bleeding. It was a slow trickle, almost an ooze. She'd been bleeding for years, she realized. Odd that she'd never taken care of it.

"People are so stupid," the girl said, "they do things and they just walk away. They think if they turn their back it isn't there anymore. That everything behind them will just go away. Disappear. Die. Dying. Dead. Dead. Dead."

That was why it was so cold all the time, Marietta realized. She must finally be going into shock.

"Nothing goes away," said the Girl intensely, "nothing ever disappears just because you don't want it."

The girl put down two cards in quick succession: Hansel and Gretel, fingers dripping, grinning mouths smeared red, the ruined body of the witch in the background. The Wolves, dashing through the snow, circling a screaming half eviscerated elk.

"Ask me my name," the girl said.

"You don't belong," Marietta said desperately, searching her hand. "You should go away, move on."

She threw down the Heaven card. It was shifting grey clouds and shadows, promising paradise.

The girl stared at the card.

Marietta looked at it again. There was nothing in its shifting texture.

"Where can I go?"

The girl was unravelling her last card, the thick wire unwound white hot and quickly cooled to a scorched metal look. She glanced up at Marietta.

Defensively Marietta spun her last card at the child.

"You aren't a ghost," she said, "You're a parasite. A psychic cancer." The card was the Lamprey.

The girl raised up her twisted wire, her mouth opened to scream, and a metallic beeping issued.

&&&

Marietta woke, feeling cold and exhausted. The metallic beeping of her phone was insistent. She stared at the clock, rubbing sleep rheum from her eyes.

She'd overslept.

Marietta answered the phone, telling her supervisor that she was sick, and begging off Hattie's next sitting this evening.

"It's all right, Marietta," her supervisor told her, "she's dead."

"What?" Marietta asked.

"She died this morning on Mabel's shift, not an hour ago."

"Oh," said Marietta. Death wasn't unexpected.

"Was there any pain?" she asked politely, uselessly.

"Died sleeping. Listen, why don't you take a couple of days, I'll call you tomorrow with the next assignment."

The receiver clicked. She hung it in the cradle.

The bedroom was unnaturally silent.

Staggering out of bed, wrapping her blankets around her for warmth, Marietta lurched to the bathroom.

Locking the door and turning on the shower, Marietta let the hot water run until it was almost scalding. She stared at herself in the mirror until it was obscured by condensation.

The heaven card, she thought, just grey and shadow.

Where had that come from?

Something to do with the dream. Forcibly, Marietta shoved the thought out of her mind and stepped into the shower.

Hot water stole her breath away for a second. She reached up to the shower head, half defensive, half supplicating. At least it was hot, blessedly hot.

Marietta stayed in the shower for what seemed like hours, washing and washing herself over again. Scraping the rough brush against her skin, letting the hot water soak her through and through, her fingers and toes shrivelling like prunes.

Finally, feeling somewhat better, she pulled on her red terrycloth bathrobe, wrapped a towel around her hair, and stepped out.

The bedroom was a mess.

Marietta was aghast. Had she done that? Perhaps, she thought. She'd been pretty sloppy the last few days. But this?

All her clothes were out of the closet, strewn randomly around. Everywhere but the bed.

She followed the trail of discarded skirts and blouses down the hall, into the living room.

The little girl, naked, was sitting cross legged on the carpet in the middle of the living room, back to Marietta, working at something. Sensing Marietta, the girl turned to look over her shoulder at her.

"Hattie was all used up," she said simply.

The girl's nimble fingers finished unstringing the coathanger. It had the seared look now. She reached for another one. The room, Marietta realized, was full of unstrung coathangers, twisted into tortured shapes, frozen in molten agony.

"You're my mommy now," the little girl sang, "forever and ever. I'm your baby, the only onliest one for ever."

The smell, Marietta realized finally, was the smell of charred flesh festering.

"We're all going to be a family together."

"Why me?" Marietta whispered.

But she knew exactly why. Regardless of whatever force inspired this thing before her, she understood now, that its face, its shape, was that of her own regrets.

The little girl held out a twisted wire, it glowed white hot, "Come and see, Mommy."

The End

Anomalous Phenomena and the Inevitability of Mass Murder as Contemplated on a Transit Bus

"They don't let nursing women fly on airplanes. That's because their breasts get so full of milk, that if the air pressure changes suddenly, they explode."

The voice was whispering and conspiratorial.

I shifted gears, the bus rumbling as I turned the corner around Wesson Street and took a peak in the rear-view to see who was telling such whoppers.

"People explode for all kinds of reasons," he was telling two wide-eyed children.

The kids were regulars on the bus. Every Saturday morning, they'd come down for the matinee movies at the mall. Eight and ten, clean cut. Obviously, they hadn't been told not to talk to strangers.

"Like if you're blood pressure gets too high, your eyeballs just burst. Pop like balloons." Some ragged old man was telling them stories. He looked like a gnome, with long wispy hair and wrinkles piled on wrinkles, so that you couldn't quite guess at his facial features. He had that threadbare groomed look that said poor but not street.

I figured he might be a perv.

Yeah, I know. That's pretty cynical. But hey, just cause he's a ninety year old fart doesn't mean he wouldn't do bad things if he had the chance.

I decided to keep an eye on him. If the kids got off at anything but their usual stop, or if he got off with them, I'd call it in.

"No!" one of the kids said.

I couldn't see their faces, but you could tell from the way they focussed on him that he had their full attention.

"Tell us more about the body on the moon!" the other one said. The younger one wasn't nearly as fascinated with exploding people stories.

I remembered the body on the moon. Something from the first or second moon landings. Buzz Armstrong finding something odd. It had been exciting at first, but nothing had ever come of it.

Odd the things you remember.

I made my stop on Smith, opening the doors and letting a half dozen Filipino ladies on. Chattering they moved to the back of the bus.

People have very definite places on the bus. I know some people; they practically have a reserved seat. If they get onto an empty bus and the only other person is sitting in their spot, they'll just stand and scowl, without even knowing why.

I used to talk about things like that, but people looked at me like I was nuts. Was it my imagination? Or are we, in spite of our conceits of free will, just relentless creatures of habit so ingrained that we won't even notice it.

From a Master's degree in Philosophy to bus driving.

Still, it wasn't a bad job.

I wasn't getting all of it, but the story he was telling was a lot more elaborate than my remembered grainy television images of Armstrong training a camera on an indistinct shape.

Made my stop on Tool road. It was a short jaunt, six blocks to Black Street, and then straight down to the Decker Mall.

I listened with half an ear, both amused and disturbed.

There was the Kennedy assassination, the secret white house tapes. Alien abductions. Mad cow disease making its way into humans. The great flu conspiracy.

You see what I mean? He was mixing fact and fiction. Telling these kids perfectly true stories, and then veering into paranoid or farcical anecdotes.

I mean: Reality is one thing. Fantasy is another. You shouldn't go mixing them. You start blurring the line for impressionable minds; god knows where they might end up.

I was just about to call him out on it. I mean, this had gone on long enough. He'd told his stories through six stops, the kids lapping it up like kittens lapping milk. He had to be a perv.

There was a donut stop on Redgrave, I had five minutes. I pulled up and set it on idle and turned around.

That's when I saw it.

Numbers tattooed across the back of his hand as he gestured.

I blushed and turned around.

A ninety year old man with numbers tattooed onto his hand. I was ashamed of myself for automatically thinking the worst. Let him have his fun, I thought, he's been through enough.

The gears ground as I jerked the bus back into life and headed for the next stop.

In the end, I had to tell the kids to get off at their stop. With effort, they pulled themselves away from the old man. He waved fondly at them as they bounced down the steps.

I'd watched him. He'd never made an improper suggestion, never touched them.

The bus was empty, except for him and me. Without the kids to animate him, he looked empty too. Small and lonely.

I cleared my throat, just to get his attention.

He looked up.

"You shouldn't tell kids those whoppers," I told him. "They'll get confused."

A strange half smile came over him.

"You were listening?"

I shrugged.

"Exploding boobs and things like that. You'll give these kids a complex."

He got up and hobbled over to me, sitting at the seat opposite the drivers, beside the door.

That made it hard for me to look at him; it was easier to scope him in the mirror. But I guess this way he could scope me.

"You know, if you hit a golf ball a certain way, it'll go off like a hand grenade. That's why everyone watches golf on Television."

I grunted.

"And if you make a face like this," he leered, "while your fingers are crossed, it'll stay like that."

I laughed.

"It's just fun," he told me, "harmless fun."

"I suppose," I said, more just to talk to him than argue, "but kids are impressionable. They can't separate the wheat from the chaff."

"That's why I talk to children," he snapped.

"Because they'll believe it?" I asked.

"How many Jews died in the Holocaust?" he asked abruptly.

"What?" I asked confused. "Shit," I said. Some asshole had cut in front of me. What did he think I was driving? A mini?

"About four and a half million," I answered.

"It could have been nine million," he said angrily.

"What?" Now he'd really lost me.

"The Nazis. They were very orderly. Efficient. The believed in bureaucracy and regulation. In getting the forms filled out, and the last detail taken care of. Orderly murder, methodical empty cruelty."

He was sinking into memory.

"I see," I said sympathetically.

"The deniers," he spat. I let it go by. "The deniers, they say only a quarter million died, like that makes it better. Even one would have been too much. They justify horror, trying to make it bland, to make it all right."

"They are trying to change history," he told me. "So am I."

"Come again?"

"Change history. I was thirty-five, a student of philosophy, like yourself..."

How did he know I'd taken philosophy, I wanted to ask.

"The world was so horrible, I wanted to unmake it. To change everything. Order had produced the Nazis, had made the world into an unending nightmare."

"After the war, I came over here, where things were better. But it didn't help. I still saw it beneath the surface. The seeds of brutality in the rules and regulations. I see a picture of a naked child running away from napalm, and I think where is the justice? It is no better. The past haunted me. I wanted to take our history and throw it into the sea."

"I can understand that," I said sympathetically.

Bitterness oozed out of him.

"Then one day, I thought why not? Why not unmake history? Perhaps this world isn't as solid as we all think. Perhaps our belief is what makes everything real."

"So I tried an experiment in nineteen sixty-four. I told someone on a bus that Oswald had not shot Kennedy."

I laughed out loud.

"Outrageous, yes?" he smiled. "But there it was. I'd started the ball rolling."

Hardly, I thought, the conspiracy theorists had been around since day one. Still, if it made him feel important, I was happy to leave him with his delusions.

"So I tried again," he said, "and again. I found that children were the best to work with. Their minds flexible, open, their world is not cast in stone."

"Children," he told me, "are the key to reality."

There was a mad-scientist glimmer in his eyes.

"But such wayward keys. Tell them a thousand stories; you never know which one will take root, spread like wildfire."

"Why do you suppose they believed that a gay man could die of a common cold? But not believe in the Library Police?" he asked.

"Sometimes," he confessed, "I feel like a dabbler. Like Doctor Mengele, all I do is carry out pointless experiments.

Perhaps I'm mad or a fool. I'll never unravel history or save
my people."

What the hell was I supposed to say?

The first thing they tell you on this job is don't talk to
nuts. Don't talk to people. Don't engage. Just do the job.

I knew why.

He reached into his pocket.

"I'll show you something," he told me. "Why I do what I
do."

He pulled out a laminated square.

I hauled into a stop. There was no one waiting.

He showed me the card.

It was a grainy newsprint photo, worn and ancient before
he'd laminated it. A ragged edge of caption identified the
naked child running down a dirt road, as a Vietnamese
refugee fleeing a napalm attack.

"The rules said that they burned children. So children
burned. There was nothing anyone could do. Children
burned. That was just the way it was."

He paused.

"Maybe if we could do something about the rules, maybe
it wouldn't be necessary that children burn. Maybe,
sometimes, children wouldn't burn."

"You're going to save the world by filling kid's minds with
exploding breasts and conspiracy theories?" I asked
incredulously.

He went stiff at that moment. Something sinister and
mean looked out his eyes. I'd heard, somewhere, that people
who survived death camps, were often, not very nice people.
The nice people died.

"What's the harm in a few stories from an old man," he
said.

He walked to the back of the bus.

End of conversation.

Don't talk to the passengers, I reminded myself.
Especially the crazy ones.

That was it. People got on, people got off. He didn't leave until nearly the end of my shift. He tried to start a few conversations with kids, but it didn't really go anywhere.

It was dark by the time I finished. I rode the bus home, a passenger. My stop was right in front of my house.

I walked in.

"You won't believe the weirdo I met today," I announced to Dorothy.

"Shhh..." she whispered. She was watching television.

Golf.

Christ, couldn't there be anything else?

Tiger Woods, the Iron Cat, stood up to Tee.

I washed up in the bathroom. When I came out, Dorothy was still watching television. She didn't even look up at me. Same damned boring routine. Nothing ever happened. We were like squirrels in a cage, trapped by habits.

"What's happening?" I asked, sitting heavily beside her.

There was carnage over the screen. A fifteen foot shallow crater out on the opening Tee, pieces of golfer and wounded spectators were all over the place.

"I hate this," I told her, "couldn't we watch something else?"

"Fitzgerald bought it on the opening drive," Dorothy said, "he barely cried 'fore' then he was gone."

The camera clipped over to interview Woods, only survivor of the Bob Hope Tournament of '98. Over twenty years playing, he'd lost an eye, his lower left leg, three fingers, five teeth and half an ear, but still he played the game.

"Damned blood sport," I grunted.

The End

Life, Love and the Necronomicon

H.P. Lovecraft wrote fiction, he never pretended otherwise. Lovecraft himself said that the Necronomicon was fiction, it was an imaginary book he occasionally referred to or made up quotes from or referred to in order to tart up his stories. Who are we to argue with that?

There shouldn't be anything more to it, or for that matter, to Howard Philips Lovecraft. He was simply one of life's failures. His father died early in life, he was raised by an attentive grandfather, a clinging mother and smothering aunts. The family fortune was lost to bad investments, the grandfather died early, and Lovecraft's mother and aunts had no skills to earn a living. Lovecraft grew up in genteel poverty, looking out on a world passing him by.

He was, by all early accounts a precocious boy. He learned to read at an early age. Although he never received formal schooling, he read voraciously. But the pressures and deficiencies of his family life took their toll, young Howard suffered a nervous breakdown at twelve, and after that, he was never quite right. He was unable to hold down a real job, and seemed unsuited for a normal life. He was married, but it didn't take. He became a writer of stories and letters, his social life, what there was of it, formed around his correspondence.

As a fiction writer, he was obscure in his time, there were literally dozens of contemporaries far more successful than him - Burroughs, Kline, Meritt, Howard, Smith, Bloch, Hubbard, Farley, some remembered, many forgotten.

Lovecraft wasn't shaking the world; he was barely eking out a living, doing the only thing he was able to do, slowly starving to death. His stories, many of which came to him in dreams, others reflecting a stark existentialist view of an alien, unsympathetic world in which humanity was a fragment, didn't quite provide a livelihood. He circled the drain, unable to make a living at the one thing he was good at, unable to do anything else. He died of cancer and should have been forgotten.

This was not an enviable man, or an enviable life. It was cramped. It was marginal. Lovecraft lived on the edges of his own existence, a cold, miserable, alienated existence. He died as he had lived his whole life, miserable, poor and alone. An unwavering trajectory that had begun in his childhood, from which he had never escaped, never found the strength or will or purpose to escape. It was as if he'd been doomed to failure and obscurity from the start.

Somehow, though, Lovecraft's cosmos, and his Necronomicon, have taken on lives of their own, appearing in short stories, novels and even movies. Enthusiastic occultists and charlatans have even published 'authentic' versions of the Necronomicon. Despite never existing, Abdul Alhazred's Necronomicon is alive and well these days, a paradox to be sure.

So let's play a game. Let's pretend that there's something to all this, that there's something authentic to the life of Lovecraft's mad poet, and that the passages attributed to him were real. Who was Abdul Alhazred, what was his life, what was true story of those mad ravings? Let us take you on a journey into...

The World of Abdul Alhazred

From H.P.Lovecraft, personal correspondence, **'The Life of Abdul Alhazred'** 1927

Quote: *"A mad poet of Sanaa, in Yemen, who is said to have flourished during the period of the Ommiad caliphs, circa 700 A.D.*

He visited the ruins of Babylon & the subterranean secret of Memphis & spent ten years alone in the great southern desert of Arabia — the Roba El Khaliyeh or "Empty Space" of the ancients — & "Dahna" or "Crimson" desert of the modern Arabs, which is held to be inhabited by protective evil spirits & monsters of death. Of this desert many strange & unbelievable marvels are told by those who pretend to have penetrated it.

In his last years Alhazred dwelt in Damascus. Of his final death or disappearance (738 A.D.) many terrible & conflicting things are told. He is said by Ebn Khallikan (12th cent. biographer) to have been seized by an invisible monster in broad daylight & devoured horribly before a large number of fright-frozen witnesses. Of his madness many things are told.

He was only an indifferent Moslem, worshiping unknown entities whom he called Yog-Sothoth & Cthulhu."

The temptation is to see and to portray Alhazred as some sort of comic book villain, cackling maniacally, scuttling around tombs, dedicated at the outset to evil for the sake of evil. He is after all the 'mad Arab' who wrote the ultimate unholy book. That probably doesn't make for a good dinner guest.

But somehow, a cartoon villain is ultimately unsatisfying. If he comes out of the womb already bad to the bone, where is there to go?

I think that there's room for a more nuanced Alhazred. More than anything, he must have been a man of his time, formed by his culture and his experiences:

If he had existed, Abdul Alhazred would certainly not have been his name. Among other things, grammatically it makes no sense in Arab culture, since the double 'al' phoneme is not proper usage.

Even beyond that, it seems unlikely that a writer of forbidden texts would publish it under his own name. More likely, Alhazred would have been a pen name, protecting the anonymity of the author. Alhazred, if he ever existed in the Arab world, would have most likely been known under a different name. Even if he was real, the name Alhazred would have been fictional.

According to Lovecraft, he died around 738 C.E., and was active around 700. If we assume he was somewhere between 20 and 50 in 700, then Alhazred's life probably began somewhere between 680 C.E, and 650 C.E. Alhazred would have been born shortly after the time of the prophet Mohammed himself, and his lifespan clearly overlapped with the original descendants and followers of Mohammed. Alhazred's history and world is that of the earliest decades of Islam, the later part of its first century, an era when traditional beliefs still held sway in many corners of Arabia.

At the age of forty, Mohammed received a revelation while meditating in a cave. Inspired, he became initially a reluctant prophet, teaching and preaching.

In 622 he relocated to Medina, becoming a political as well as religious leader. Through wars, conquests and conversions, he had united the entire Arabian Peninsula under Islam by 632. Conquests followed relentlessly after that. Syria fell in 633. Palestine in 637. Egypt in 641. Libya in 644. The entire Persian Empire fell in 646. Within little more than a decade of Mohammed's death, the great Empires of the day, the Persian and Roman had literally been swept aside in a stunning wave of conquests.

More conquests would follow, a generation letter, by 677, Tunisia and Algeria fell, followed within a few years by Morocco and Spain by 711.

By the time of Alhazred, Islam had spread from a local cult in the city of Medina to a world spanning Empire whose borders extended from France to India. But it was a young empire in every sense of the world, its rule was light.

How did this happen?

Before Mohammed, the Arabian Peninsula was a backwater, its interior occupied by roving nomadic tribes of horsemen and camel traders, its southern coasts and northern oasis dotted with agricultural settlements, even cities and towns. They had been around for thousands of years; they'd developed their own culture, their own gods, even their own system of writing. Some of them were nomadic Bedouin, some were barbarian equivalents of the western barbarians or Mongols, some were city dwellers, merchants and traders at the level of Greeks and Phoenicians. They were peoples of diverse lifestyles, literate, accomplished, and squabbling.

But they had never amounted to anything substantial. Empires and civilizations, the Egyptians, the Babylonians, the Persians, Phoenicians and Greeks flourished struggled around them, but they were minor pawns in the story, with no indication that they would ever be anything more.

Rome had in the time of Caesar brought a peace to the Mediterranean world. But for the technology and communications, the world was just too big and scattered to control from one city. Roman administration was divided between east and west, between Rome and Constantinople. Secondary centers were established at Carthage and Alexandria. Rome fell; the eastern side, ruled from Constantinople simply kept on going, and became the Byzantine Empire, somewhere around the fourth century.

For the Romans and Byzantines, the big rival was the Persian Empire. Each Empire was continually building and abandoning fortresses along an ever shifting border, preparatory to invading or defending. The Persians fortunes waxed and waned as dynasties came and went. They contended with the Romans over the whole of the Middle East, entire countries changing hands from one dynasty to the next.

But we're getting ahead of ourselves. The Byzantines in the sixth century under Justinian embarked on the reconquest of the western half of the former Roman Empire. They managed to regain Italy, North Africa, some of Spain. But in the end, the struggle bankrupted and exhausted both armies and treasuries. For a time, Justinian kept the Persians out of his hair by bribing them. That wasn't going to last. Justinian's successors stopped paying.

Early in the seventh century, the Persians attacked, conquering Syria, Palestine, the coasts of Arabia and even Egypt, by 622 the Byzantines were on the verge of collapse.

The Byzantines counterattacked, the tides of war and conquest shifted, and they took it all back, by 627.

But the struggle left both Empires near bankrupt, their treasuries depleted, their economies crippled, populations exhausted and their armies decimated. Egypt and Syria had changed hands back and forth three times in the previous decade.

The Persians, defeated, went through a series of temporary and impotent rulers. The Byzantines were unable to follow up on their hair's breadth victory; they were fighting Avars and Bulgars in the Balkans and Lombard Barbarians in Italy. Their struggles had exhausted both empires, had bled them white.

All of this would be normal fun and games, except for what was going on in the south. In the middle of Arabia a man named Mohammed emerged, preaching the doctrine of one true God. For the first time in history the squabbling, fractious, diverse peoples of the Arabian Peninsula were united under one faith and one government.

By the time of his death in 632, his followers had conquered most of Arabia, and they were ready to break out big time.

Normally, that wouldn't have mattered. A unified Arabia would have been a minor power compared to either the Persians or Byzantines at full strength. But it was the perfect storm. The two big Empires had just, at that time, pounded each other to rubble.

At the very moment these two great Empires were at their weakest, Islam burst into existence upon the perfect, golden historical moment to emerge and sweep them aside, to forge something completely new and unforeseen literally overnight.

For once, these new inheritors could handle it. The Arabs were not just nomadic horsemen; they were traders, artisans, scholars and city dwellers. For centuries, they'd been on the pathways between Asia and Europe, Africa and Asia. Their sailors and merchants were part of trading networks that reached down to the coastlines of southern Africa and the fringes of China. They had the bloodthirsty martial valor to conquer an Empire and the sophistication to rule it.

This gives us our first window into Alhazred. Born in Arabia, the center of Mohamed's faith, a product of the civilized southern Yemeni reaches, he was almost certainly a devout Muslim, at least at the outset.

His relocations to Damascus, to Egypt, to Damascus and Babylon are not the wanderings of a mad demon worshiper but journeys within the Muslim world, to its centers of culture and civilization.

Indeed, many of the writings attributed to Alhazred and the Necronomicon seems far more consistent with those of a devout Muslim rather than a mad mystic.

Journey Into the Abyss

From H.P. Lovecraft's short story., '**The Festival**.' 1923

Quote: *"The nethermost caverns are not for the fathoming of eyes that see; for their marvels are strange and terrific. Cursed the ground where dead thoughts live new and oddly bodied, and evil the mind that is held by no head.*

Wisely did Ibn Schacabao say, that happy is the tomb where no wizard hath lain, and happy the town at night whose wizards are all ashes. For it is of old rumor that the soul of the devil-bought hastes not from his charnel clay, but fats and instructs the very worm that gnaws; till out of corruption horrid life springs, and the dull scavengers of earth wax crafty to vex it and swell monstrous to plague it.

Great holes are digged where earth's pores ought to suffice, and things have learnt to walk that ought to crawl."

Creepy as hell, is it not?

But what do we suppose Alhazred is really talking about here?

Observe that there's no sign of Cthulhu, Azathoth or whatnot. The Ancient Ones do not make an appearance. There are no portentous hints of other dimensions. Indeed, the passage is almost prosaic in its concerns.

What are those concerns? He's talking mostly about tombs.

Quote: 'Nethermost caverns that are not for ... eyes that see', in other words, resting places for the dead. 'Tombs' for wizards, priests and powerful devil-bought infidels. 'Charnel clay' where the dead do not rot away as they should.

That failure to decompose properly is an obvious tip off. Alhazred is discoursing about Egypt. Those bodies that do not rot away? He's talking about the process or tradition of mummification where the flesh of the dead is preserved for millennia.

And more, he's ranting about the practice of storing the dead in tunnels or caves or elaborate tombs, even mighty pyramids, which protect them from the ravages of decay.

He's talking about Egypt, and the burial and funereal practices of ancient Egyptian society, practices that are deeply alien to him and his culture.

Seriously, if he's going to be obsessing and raving on about tombs, where else could he possibly be?

But why? What concerns him?

Because he sees it as dangerous. He's a provincial Arab Muslim, and Egyptian society and ways are alien to him, and alien in his eyes can only mean 'against Allah' or unholy and blasphemous.

Alhazred is a scion of an empire only a generation or so old. His culture has only recently emerged from the Arabian Peninsula.

And here he is plopped down in the center of a civilization thousands of years old, a civilization whose Pyramids and giant megaliths tower over him everywhere he looks. The Arabs were familiar with Egypt, and had dealt with the Egyptians for millennia.

But that's quite a different thing than suddenly finding oneself standing in front of the Pyramid of Cheops, or the Sphinx, confronting the Valley of the Kings or the various necropolises.

Alhazred's was a pre-scientific society. Faced with immense structures beyond the scale of anything he had known, pyramids, statues, obelisks, columns, tombs and temples, he could only assume that magic was at work.

Magic, by definition in Allah's brave new world, was the product of congress with unholy demons. There was no god but Allah, all those other so called Gods, could only be demons.

To a Muslim of Alhazred's time, whoever these ancient Egyptians had been, they were obviously formidable sorcerers, only fearsome sorcery could be responsible for the cyclopean architecture he sees.

The sorcerers of Egypt are all dead now, clearly defeated by the righteousness of Allah and his followers.

But the very relics, the remains, the vast temples and tombs, their simple continuing existence is disturbing.

But Alhazred warns that their demonic powers may yet reside within their tombs, a kind of series of supernatural land mines or unexploded bombs, waiting to go off. Evil the mind (forbidden knowledge) not contained by a head (control or wisdom). Dead thoughts pose a danger if they find their way into new forms

So what's all this talk of pores in the earth, or things that crawl learning to walk?

Grave robbers.

Alhazred is practical. He knows that the tombs, left to themselves are mostly harmless. So where's the danger? The danger is tomb raiders, bandits, grave robbers.

As Alhazred sees it, the risk is criminals and scum, thugs and revolutionaries, those who ought to be crawling before Allah and his faithful.

If they get in and batten on the forbidden demonic lore, they may become a threat. They who ought to crawl, men who are the scum of the earth, may wind up walking, if they obtain forbidden knowledge from these tombs.

The Alhazred depicted in these passages is at the beginning of his journey. He's still a devout Muslim, even a narrow-minded priggish Muslim, one who has moved from Arabia to Egypt. He's astonished by the monuments, the obvious antiquity, yet the burial practices repel him as acts of demonic idolatry.

In this passage, he is a loyal, somewhat pedantic, servant of the Caliphate, sounding the alarm about a potential supernatural or political threat.

The Seduction of Memphis

From H.P. Lovecraft & E. Hoffman Price, novella **"Through the Gates of the Silver Key'** 1923-1933)

Quote: *"And while there are those who have dared to seek glimpses beyond the Veil, and to accept HIM as a Guide, they would have been more prudent had they avoided commerce with HIM; for it is written in the Book of Thoth how terrific is the price of a single glimpse. Nor may those who pass ever return, for in the Vastnesses transcending our world are Shapes of darkness that seize and bind.*

The Affair that shambleth about in the night, the Evil that defieth the Elder Sign, the Herd that stand watch at the secret portal each tomb is known to have, and that thrive on that which groweth out of the tenants within -- all these Blacknesses are lesser than HE Who guardeth the Gateway; HE Who will guide the rash one beyond all the worlds into the Abyss of unnamable Devourers. For HE is UMR AT-TAWIL, the Most Ancient One, which the scribe rendereth as THE PROLONGED OF LIFE."

Where is Alhazred at the time of this writing?

The reference to the Book of Thoth tells us several things. Obviously, at the time this was written, Alhazred is still in Egypt and still obsessed with the evidence of the past that looms over everything.

Let's go back to the big picture for a second.

In 640, the Islamic Jihad had overrun Egypt. Big deal. By this time, the Egyptians were pretty used to being conquered. The glory days of their own Empire were long past. Since then, they'd been overrun by Nubians, Hittites, Persians, Alexanders Greeks, Romans, Persians again, and Byzantines. Through it all, the Egyptians had retained their timeless traditions, and their ancient gods and temples. The rulers might change, but Egyptian society did not.

The original Egyptian capital had been Memphis, city of Pharaohs and monuments. When Alexander came in, he founded Alexandria, which became the new capital city for the Greek dynasty of the Ptolemy's for the later Roman rule and governance. But Memphis persisted as a major city and center of Egyptian culture. When Christianity came along in the second and third centuries it established itself in Alexandria, leaving Memphis as the center of the old religions.

The Arabs, when they conquered Egypt in 640 decided to have no truck or trade with Memphis, or with Alexandria for that matter.

Instead, they decided to build their own capital city. The story is that Amr Ibn Al-As, the general who conquered Egypt decided to build a city where his tent was. The city was called Fustat, and became the Arabic political and administrative capital of Egypt in 641. Another Arab town founded slightly later, Cairo in 648 eventually came to merge with and dominate Fustat. Nowadays, what was once Fustat is known simply as 'Old Cairo.' Even its name was devoured by its rival.

I'm not sure why the Arabs decided to build a brand new city when there were a whole bunch of them perfectly serviceable cities available. It may have been for military purposes, or perhaps for bureaucratic or administrative reasons.

But if you ask me, I think Memphis just freaked them out. This was Egypt. This was the place they built the Pyramids. Dozens of them, and horking big ones. This was the place with the Sphinx, the Valley of the Kings, and the Saqqara Necropolis. It had Obelisks and Libraries with hundreds of thousands of books. There were twenty and fifty foot statues, just lying around, like the Egyptians had run out of places to put the damned things. The Egyptians were so lousy with monuments and cyclopean architecture that they'd just forget about the sphinx and let it get buried. Even their ditches, the

ancient canal connecting the Mediterranean to the Red were
colossal. It had cities that were thousands of years old. Cities
that existed, had risen, had fallen; long before Allah's name
was ever spoken.

.You face all that, well, it was just hard to deal with.
Maybe, if you were truly serious about Mohammed being the
prophet, well, maybe you just didn't want to deal with it.

Whatever the reason, Memphis was largely abandoned. It
was no accident, but a decision that had to be some sort of
deliberate Islamic policy. Memphis became a source of stone,
raw materials cannibalized to build the new cities of Cairo and
Fustat.

Alhazred at this point in his life has clearly not begun to
evolve his own gods and cosmology. That will come. Thoth
will become Azathoth and Yog-Sothoth, but that's obviously
still in the future, and he is still dealing with Thoth in his
Egyptian form.

Alhazred as depicted here is clearly writing about
Egyptian afterlife beliefs which he deems unholy, and
contrasting them with the holy writ of Allah. Egyptian
mysticism promises a glimpse into the afterlife, but what an
awful price for such a glimpse, to be judged by a Jackal
headed being and then damned to a whole menagerie of
baboons and crocodiles and a hippo that devours the
unworthy.

But Alhazred's position has evolved. In the previous
passage he was condemning ancient lore out of hand without
knowing much about it, warning of its potential danger and
all but demanding that it be put to the torch. But prudery
always demands encroachment. One can only denounce
pornography for so long before the urge becomes to examine
and study the offending material, so better to denounce it.

Alhazred is no longer condemning from a safe distance.
He's begun to study it in detail, learning more about the
heresies and blasphemies he seeks to confront. He seeks to
understand it to raise arguments against it, to better oppose it.

Alhazred, despite his devotion to the faith, has become a
student of other faiths, a seeker into other mysteries, if only

to conclusively rebut and destroy them once and for all. He studies to expose them, to expose their lies and deceits and thus elevate the truth of Allah.

He's wading into deeper waters, but he's still a good Muslim in his own mind.

But where is Alhazred?

We don't know exactly when Alhazred was supposed to have been in Egypt. But it would be at least a generation or two after the founding of Cairo and Fustat. The new Arabic cities would be well established and thriving. Memphis would have been all but a dead city, with the dagger planted in its heart for generations.

Still, the city would have been glorious. Even as late as the 12th century, it was apparently an imposing set of ruins. Here in the first generations of its ruins, it would be largely intact. The monuments, the temples, the great traditional buildings would have been all intact or at worst only partly deconstructed. It might have been like walking through a ghost town, some streets completely intact, others half unbuilt, the absence of crowds everywhere.

And yet, it would have been a ghost town of immense antiquity, inhabited only by the most hard core, full of incredibly ancient temples and statuary, and literally a gateway to immense and ancient structures, like the Pyramids of Giza and Saqqara. It could have only been an awesome and stunning experience.

The only inhabitants would have been sullen and withdrawn, strange resentful natives clinging to the old ways, and of course the quarriers, dismantling building after building for its stone. One can imagine the Coptic Christian Church would have had a stronghold in Alexandra. But Memphis was an even older and more traditional city full of ruins and relics. If anything was left of the old priesthoods and temples of Egypt, it was going to be here.

Egypt was a very different place thirteen hundred years ago. The Islamic movement had conquered Egypt, but did not yet own it. The population at this point had been under Roman and Byzantine rule for a half millennium; it had been under Greek influence for a half millennium before that. Christianity had taken hold of only a few centuries, and part of Christianity's strength had been the enforcement of the state. It was a center of the Gnostic schools. And beneath it all was the old traditions, the old temples, the old ways. Who knows what lay seething beneath the surface of Arab rule?

We know that the old Egyptian religion hung on for a time, but the belief is that Coptic Christianity displaced and replaced the old temples relatively quickly. I'm not so sure of this myself. It strikes me that the traditional temples and gods were durable repositories of Egyptian culture. It had endured for millennia, in evolving forms. And there was likely political and economic capital tied up in those temples.

The Egyptian religions were undoubtedly subordinated to the Christian Church, particularly from the third century on, when Christianity was the official religion of the Roman and later Byzantine Empires. But Christianity under the Byzantines was a Greek religion. So my thinking is that in some subordinated form, the Egyptians who had endured so many conquerors clung to the old ways.

If the old religions had survived to the coming of Islamic rule, they would have experienced a temporary rejuvenation. Once Mohamed's followers came in Christianity was no longer the official state religion. The Arabs, initially, had no special interest in converting infidels to the faith. Indeed, they were leery of the idea. Allah was just for them, you start letting every Tom, Dick and Harry into the faith, well, who knows where things will end up? Believe it or not, in those days, the only way to become a Muslim was to marry into an Arab family. The expansion of the faith came gradually, and with no few reservations. They were particularly dubious about all the Persians joining the faith in those days.

So it's likely that with the old state religion deposed, and the new state religion reluctant to accept applicants, the first decades after the Islamic conquest may have actually seen a short lived revival of the traditional Egyptian faiths. A development that the Islamic conquerors might have had mixed feelings about.

The center of the old ways would have been in Memphis. Thus, it seems likely that when Alhazred is writing about the Book of Thoth and denouncing the Egyptian afterlife as a passage to devouring unnameable demons, he is doing so in the dying city of Memphis.

He is confronting the unknown on its own territory.

And in the end, he loses.

The Sorcerer and the Crisis of Faith

From Clark Ashton Smith's short story, '**The Return of the Sorcerer**' 1931

Quote: *"It is verily known by few, but is nevertheless no attestable fact, that the will of a dead sorcerer hath power upon his own body and can raise it up from the tomb and perform therewith whatever action was unfulfilled in life. And such resurrections are invariably for the doing of malevolent deeds and for the detriment of other's.*

Most readily can the corpse be animated if all its members have remained intact; and yet there are cases in which the excelling will of the wizard hath reared up from death the sundered pieces of a body hewn in many fragments, and hath caused them to serve his end, either separately or in a temporary reunion. But in every instance, after the action hath been completed, the body lapseth into its former state.

This is nothing more and nothing less than Alhazred's righteous attack upon the blasphemy Christianity itself.

A dead sorcerer whose will reanimates his own corpse to fulfill some evil purpose? Alhazred here gives us his opinion of the Christian miracle of the resurrection. It is not the hand of god or the proof of Christ's divinity; it is merely a sorcerer's trick.

And in fact, the sorcerer's trick is not confined to the miracle of the resurrection. It extends to body parts. This is a direct reference to the then well-established Christian practice of veneration of holy relic, particularly the bones and body parts of saints and holy men.

During the middle ages, literally every major Christian temple or church could lay claim to some piece of a dismembered saint. Alhazred is pretty much attributing this practice to the same sort of sorcery that lies behind the miracle of the resurrection.

Where does Alhazred get this notion? From Egyptian religious and burial practices obviously. It's clear that Alhazred has by this time delved quite deeply into Egyptian lore, that he understands the Egyptian belief in an afterlife and the need for physical remains. He seems confused by the Egyptian's emphasis on providing foodstuffs and furnishings for those remains, as if they're expected to return to life. And he's aware of, but not fully understanding, the ancient practice of exhuming (dismembering) the corpse and keeping the organs in jars. Alhazred has learned something of the Egyptian practices, though his understanding is crude and distorted.

To him it's all sorcery and devil worship. Repulsive stuff, mired in evil, antithetical to the clean light of Allah's divinity. He's coming to understand sorcerers and their ways.

And there is the problem.

Because when he looks at Christianity, and at this point in history, Egypt is full of Christians. Islam has not yet taken over the population, the land is Christian, the beliefs are Christian. Christian lore and legends proliferate. And just below them the old faiths.

Railing against the old faiths, Alhazred cannot help but see the underlying connections and interweavings between those who worship the cross, and those who practice ancient ways. He comes to see the lore and traditions of Christianity as drawing on the ways of sorcerers. Once he starts to see the connections, he can't unsee them.

Alhazred comes to see the Christian story of the resurrection as simply more Egyptian necromancy, tarted up for the masses, sold as divinity. But he sees through it. He sees that Christ was nothing more than a filthy sorcerer, his miracles mere cheap demonic tricks.

Jesus is revealed to Alhazred as a false messiah, a false deity, a false prophet. The Christian faith is simply superstition and devil worship.

Without realizing it, Alhazred's zealotry is driving him to apostasy.

You see, Jesus is not just part of the Christian faith.

The Koran recognizes Jesus Christ as a bona fide prophet, not a sorcerer.

But the Koran is the absolute and infallible word of god.

Except … Jesus is a filthy sorcerer, a trickster, not a prophet. Alhazred knows this in his bones, everything he's learned studying the superstitions and idolatry of Egypt points to it.

But…if Jesus is a sorcerer and not a prophet, then the Koran is wrong. The Koran is not infallible. Not the absolute and inerrant word of Allah.

Now the cracks are running through his faith. He faces contradiction, where once he had the rock of certainty.

If the Koran is fallible, if it is fallible about Jesus, what else has it gotten wrong? This is the beginning of the crisis of faith.

Alhazred stand there in Egypt, in a land of statues and monoliths, of tombs and temples ancient beyond all human comprehension.

Alhazred thought he knew the world, he thought he had the answers, he thought his faith was all he needed, that his faith was all there was.

Except here he is, that faith is riven with a contradiction, a paradox. And beyond that, the world around him is so much larger, and vaster than he's ever imagined. Everywhere he looks, he sees the evidence of cyclopean monuments, and incomprehensible age, the evidence of peoples and places and things he's never imagined, he's never imagined that he could even imagine these things.

A world infinitely vaster than he's ever conceived. A world where Allah and his faith and his world are small and transient things.

Alhazred's inquiring mind, his dedication, has brought him to the point he cannot turn away from. And there is a moment, somewhere out there, his faith shatters, and with it his mind.

He goes mad.

The Madman in the Desert

From H.P. Lovecraft, **Private Letters**, speaking of Alhazred

Quote: *"He claimed to have seen the fabulous Irem, or City of Pillars, & to have found beneath the ruins of a certain nameless desert town the shocking annals & secrets of a race older than mankind.*

What happens when a good man breaks? When his faith is broken, when the pillars by which he has lived his life are shattered? When everything he thought was sane and normal and just is taken away?

What does he do?

Alhazred had gone into the world as a man of faith, a devout Muslim, a worshipper of Allah, confident that his God had made the world.

And yet, he had encountered apostasy, vast and ancient ruins older than time itself. Unnatural practices, corpses preserved against eternity, tombs that dominated the sky, sorcerers that reanimated themselves. At first, it appalled and disgusted him; he sought to confront it, to rebut it.

But steadily, it broke him.

He could not bear it. He flees.

So he returned home, to Yemen, to the south of Arabia.

But this was not an escape, because he carried within him what he had seen. His home the world he'd known was now trivial and evanescent, a passing shadow to what he'd seen.

And so he did what broken men always do.

He flees again, this time away from his home, away from the world he knows, away from humanity, into the desert, to dwell in Irem.

Irem appears in the Koran, a counterpart to Atlantis and Sodom and Gomorrah. It was a proud city whose citizens fell to selfishness and wickedness, so Allah sent a great sandstorm and the Earth swallowed it up.

But there really was an Irem, known as Ubar. In the 21st century, satellites located it, tracking ancient camel paths. What they found in those ancient tracks was something like a road, or roads, converging on a place that no longer existed.

Irem, or Ubar, was a trading post in the great desert, a watering hole. Caravans passed through steadily. It became a walled compound and market, guarded by seven great stone towers. The population waxed and waned as caravans came and went, and travellers bided for a spell. Perhaps it reached hundreds, maybe thousands.

To the wandering nomads of the desert and their trading caravans, Ubar must have seemed a wondrous place with its magnificent towers, with the markets within its sturdy walls and throngs camping outside, fabulously wealthy as a commercial center will become, a place of art and licentiousness.

And there was something else.

It was called the 'City of Pillars'?

What does that mean?

In the Pre-Muslim era, the Arabs worshipped a pantheon of gods. These gods were represented by a stone or pillar, not unlike the Kaaba, and worshippers would walk a circle around their god's pillar, chanting and praying.

When Arabia converted to monotheism, the followers of Allah went about with hammers, smashing the pillars of these false gods. But this would come much later.

Irem was a metropolitan center in the desert. Different caravans, different tribes came through, some stayed. They brought their gods with them, in the form of stone pillars. A stone pillar was often carried on journeys, but quite often, it was easier to leave or raise a pillar in a safe area, a place you knew you'd return to again and again.

And so Irem became a city of pillars, of standing stones raised to members of the pre-Islamic pantheon. It became a city where every tribe had its god.

This is what the Koran really means when it refers to Irem as a city of pillars. Not pillars in the Greek sense. Rather, within the Koran, in the eyes of Muslims, Irem had

been a demon haunted city. It had earned the destruction
Allah had visited upon it.

Here is a point where legend merges with fact.

Irem really was swallowed up by a sandstorm, fell into the
earth.

You see, Irem was an oasis in the desert, that was its
foundation. There was a huge underground limestone aquifer
that supplied water to the locals, and to passing caravans, that
perhaps even supported a bit of agriculture and a great deal of
commerce.

But year by year, that water had been drawn. Decade
upon decade thousands and thousands of inhabitants, of
caravans and passing tribes, tens or hundreds of thousands of
beasts and humans. The waters drew down and down, until
literally, the city was perched atop a great empty vault.

One night a sandstorm blew up, and Irem opened its
gates to give shelter to caravans. Imagine that night, the sky
roaring, the air thick with stinging blasting sand, visibility
reduced to nothing.

Then all of a sudden, the world gives way. The entire city
literally falls into a great sinkhole. Imagine the shock and
terror, the earth opening up to swallow everyone and
everything.

When it was all over, the survivors crawled back into the
sunlight, to stare blinking and uncomprehending. Where only
hours before there'd been a great walled city with towers and
markets, there was only a chasm in the earth, filled with
bodies, the calls and moans of trapped and injured people and
animals rising up.

The survivors went away. No one ever came to Irem
again; there was no more worship at its famed pillars. The
place was cursed, its waters now inaccessible. The Caravans
went elsewhere.

But the stories persisted and found their way into the
Koran.

Archeology verifies the story of Irem. In modern terms, it
was probably not so much; it seems to have been a small
place ultimately. But look back through time; look through

the eyes of desert nomads, of caravans and weary travellers. I must have been marvelous, and when it fell, it must have seemed like the world itself falling into the abyss.

This is where Alhazred found himself. Or perhaps he sought it out. Where else would you go to seek out your faith, than a place where God had worked his will. Even today, Christians go searching for the remnants of Noah's Ark, or the sites of Sodom and Gomorrah, seeking the evidence of God's wrath.

Today, there is nothing left of Irem.

But remember Alhazred's era was perhaps barely more than a few decades or centuries after the fall of era. What he found was very different than what we'd see today.

The walls and towers would have still been partially intact, the pillars raised to supplanted gods, some of them still remaining. The sink hole would have been a chasm, filled with skeletons of humans and animals, still with traces of water in its depths supporting snakes and scorpions and perhaps even a few hardy souls.

This is what Alhazred would have found, deep in the chasm, water and sustenance enough to live on, the ruins of a demon haunted city, the relics of a charnel house.

In this place, if he was searching for the wise and beneficent Allah, he did not find it.

Instead, once again, he was confronted with antiquity, with a world vaster and more alien than he had ever imagined could exist. A world in which he and everything he'd believed was irrelevant, a passing fancy.

Alhazred had fled Egypt, fled the wonders and terrors of world vaster and stranger than he'd ever imagined. He'd fled back home to Arabia. Ultimately, he'd fled into the desert searching for Allah.

And instead, he'd found only the abyss.

A deeper madness.

The Terror of the Abyss

From H.P. Lovecraft's story, **'The Dunwich Horror,'** 1928)

"Nor is it to be thought, that man is either the oldest or the last of earth's masters, or that the common bulk of life and substance walks alone. The Old Ones were, the Old Ones are, and the Old Ones shall be. Not in the spaces we know, but between them,

They walk serene and primal, undimensioned and to us unseen. Yog-Sothoth knows the gate. Yog-Sothoth is the gate. Yog-Sothoth is the key and guardian of the gate. Past, present, future, all are one in Yog-Sothoth. He knows where the Old Ones broke through of old, and where They shall break through again. He knows where They have trod earth's fields, and where They still tread them, and why no one can behold Them as They tread.

By Their smell can men sometimes know Them near, but of Their semblance can no man know, saving only in the features of those They have begotten on mankind; and of those are there many sorts, differing in likeness from man's truest eidolon to that shape without sight or substance which is Them. They walk unseen and foul in lonely places where the Words have spoken and the Rites howled through at their Seasons. The wind gibbers with Their voices, and the earth mutters with Their consciousness. They bend the forest and crush the city, yet may not forest or city behold the hand that smites.

Kadath in the cold waste hath known Them, and what man knows Kadath? The ice desert of the South and the sunken isles of Ocean hold stones whereon Their seal is engraven, but who hath seen the deep frozen city or the sealed tower long garlanded with seaweed and barnacles?

Great Cthulhu is Their cousin, yet can he spy Them only dimly. Iä! Shub-Niggurath!

As a foulness shall ye know Them.

Their hand is at your throats, yet ye see Them not.

Their habitation is even one with your guarded threshold.

Yog-Sothoth is the key to the gate, whereby the spheres meet.

Man rules now where They ruled once; They shall soon rule where man rules now. After summer is winter, and after winter summer. They wait patient and potent, for here shall They rule again."

This passage is replete with existential terror. Alhazred has lost it completely. He's gone mad. This is a broken man raging and raving in the desert.

Existential Fear drives his language. Consider the hysterical repetition, the obsessiveness of terror.

Quote: 'Yog-Sothoth knows the gate. Yog-Sothoth is the gate. Yog-Sothoth is the key and guardian of the gate. Past, present, future, all are one in Yog-Sothoth.'

The constant repetition is like a religious liturgy. But more than that, it speaks to Yog-Sothoth's magical omnipotence. Whatever the gate is, Yog-Sothoth rules it completely. Yog-Sothoth owns that gate, and it's not a good thing.

Alhazred is not worshipping the old ones here, rather, they frighten of him. Allah is a figment, he no longer believes, but this does not bring him peace, but rather unimaginable horror. The writing speaks of apocalyptic terror.

One imagines him raving in the Arabian Desert, consumed by his primordial horror.

Here, finally, the Gods of the Necronomicon make their appearance.

Here we find Azathoth, Yog-Sothoth, Shub-Niggurath, Cthulhu. But what really terrifies Alhazred is infinity, a vast reality unbounded and infinite, terrifying in its immensity.

Quote: "...man is neither the oldest nor the last of earth's masters... Kadath in the cold waste hath known Them, and what man knows Kadath? The ice desert of the South and the sunken isles of Ocean hold stones whereon Their seal is engraven, but who hath seen the deep frozen city or the sealed tower long garlanded with seaweed and barnacles? ...Their habitation is even one with your guarded threshold..... After summer is winter, and after winter summer. They wait patient and potent, for here shall They rule again."

If religion arises from man confronting his own mortality, Alhazred is confronting the mortality of his own religion. Alhazred was suffering the awful conception that Allah was finite, not the architect of the universe, but merely a passing season. That his faith was finite.

That there had been a world and gods before Allah, that there would be a world and gods after Allah, and the even now, there was a world and gods beyond Allah. That there had, inescapably been entire races, civilisations, cities before his time, and that there would be ones after. That everything he thought was real and permanent in the world, was just a passing season, and that the traces and ruins of prior worlds were all about.

Imagine the crushing religious terror.

At Irem the abyss howled before Alhazred, and unable to face naked infinity, he peopled it with his own gods, gods that reflected his terror and despair.

Quote: "...the Old Ones broke through of old, and where They shall break through again. .... They walk unseen and foul in lonely places where the Words have spoken and the Rites howled through at their Seasons. They bend the forest and crush the city, yet may not forest or city behold the hand that smites. .... As a foulness shall ye know Them."

The scent of the ancient charnel house in the sinkhole at Irem, stale water and limestone and ancient decay.

Quote: "Their hand is at your throats, yet ye see Them not; and Their habitation is even one with your guarded threshold. ......Man rules now where They ruled once; They shall soon rule where man rules now.... They wait patient and potent, for here shall They rule again."

Perhaps these were the genuine products of Alhazred's syncretic ravings, or merely the perversions of names of existing Gods. It didn't matter. For the first time the gods of the Necronomicon's pantheon emerge: Yog-Sothoth, Shub-Niggurath, Cthulhu.

The Gnosticism

From Ramsay Campbell's short story, **'The Plain of Sound'** 1965

Quote: *"Verily do we know little of the other universes beyond the gate which Yog-Sothoth guards. Of those which come through the gate and make their habitation in this world none can tell; although Ibn Schacabao tells of the beings which crawl from the Gulf of S'glhuo that they may be known by their sound. In that Gulf the very worlds are of sound, and matter is known but as an odor; and the notes of our pipes in this world may create beauty or bring forth abominations in S'glhuo. For the barrier between haply grows thin, and when sourceless sounds occur we may justly look to the denizens of S'glhuo. They can do little harm to those of Earth and fear only that shape which a certain sound may form in their universe."*

Clearly madness consumed him. Another man might have spent his life raving and mad in the ruins of Irem, subsisting on snakes and scorpions, living alongside the impoverished descendants of the survivors.

But Alhazred was an educated man, a sophisticated one, and even if his faith was broken, he himself was not. Or at least, he would not remain broken. He left Irem to seek out civilization. His homelands in Yemen no longer suited him, Egypt was too forbidding. Inevitably, he was drawn to the center of Muslim thought and learning, to Damascus.

It was there that his search for meaning brought him to the remnants of Gnosticism.

It was here that he wrote of S'glhuo, with clearly mixed emotions, revulsion and religious antipathy mixed with inquiry and curiouslity. It contains much of his evolved thought.

The marks of his journey are plain in his writing. Very clear is the notion that our world is a limited place, and that there are other places beyond and other beings which are utterly alien to us. Yog-Sothoth appears as a character.

He is still struggling with his religious crisis, but now in a thoughtful, metaphorical way. His descriptions of the inhabitants of S'glhuo and their relationship to us clearly is intended to parallel our relationships to the old ones. Like the old ones to us, we are invisible to S'glhuo. As we know the old ones by their odor, so too does S'glhuo know us by our odor. As S'glhuo is immaterial and unreal to us, so too are we unreal and immaterial to the old ones. Pipes and the sound of pipes are recurring imagery connected to the Old Ones in the Lovecraft's stories, whereas in S'glhuo it is us who are tied to the pipes.

We can, through bare effort, playing pipes, bring beauty or abomination to their world. And thus, by the same token, the Old Ones are dangerous to us....

But not necessarily so.

We, as alien beings, offer beauty and abomination to the S'glhuo. So too, as alien beings do the Old Ones offer the options of abomination and beauty.

Indeed, it appears that the tale of S'glhuo represents Alhazred's effort to come to grips with his concept of the Old Ones, a concept which has reduced him to gibbering terror and madness. He does this by using the S'glhuo as a kind of metaphor, allowing him to handle notions that he can't face directly. Using the S'glhuo as a kind of distancing tool, he allows himself to see the greater universe as alien rather than antithetical. Clearly he's calmed down and he's not wandering in the desert any more raving like a madman.

It is interesting how closely his S'glhuo metaphor parallels Gnostic thought.

The Gnostics were a lost religious tradition, from the early Christian era. There were several schools of Gnostic belief; particularly important groups were in Egypt and in Damascus.

Gnosis was Greek for knowledge, and the Gnostics pursued a path of personal enlightenment.

In a nutshell, the Gnostics believed in a remote and unknowable supreme being, removed from the Universe, but from whom humans received a spark of the divine.

Unfortunately, as the Supreme Being created other beings, they grew steadily more imperfect, resulting in a 'demi-urge', a sort of deformed, buffoonish and slightly sadistic being who creates our universe.

The Gnostic demi-urge is equivalent to the Jehovah of the Judaic and Christian faiths, and is intended to explain why the god of the Old Testament is such a capricious prick.

Humanity and the world we live in are the flawed and inferior creations of a flawed and inferior creator, a degraded, washed out photocopy of the celestial world of the true Supreme Being.

The metaphor the Gnostics used was one of art – this degraded world we lived in, was like a painting compared to the true world, an imperfect flat representation.

But the Gnostics believed that because humans held a spark of the divine, and that through study and enlightenment we could transcend this world of muck and horror, escape the clutches of the insane Old Testament gosling and join the divine realm.

Jesus Christ and his apostles appeared as savior or teacher in many of the Gnostic sects, making them nominally Christian. However, Gnosticism emphasized enlightenment and discipline on an individual basis rather than faith as in mainstream Christianity. Put it this way, the Gnostics were not joiners, they didn't believe in congregations, so the more popular Christian faith won out.

The Gnostics were once presumed to have been wiped out by the end of the second century, but discovery of the Nag Hammadi scrolls confirm that their movement endured at least through the fourth century.

It's now believed that they may well have survived into the Islamic period, and some later traditions, such as the Cathars of Medieval France may well be derived from Gnostic traditions. And so Alhazred, as he searched for enlightenment would find them in Damascus.

Even in their heyday, the Gnostics were pretty hard going. As a faith, or philosophy, they weren't interested in proselytizing or gaining converts. They did not preach revelation, but rather, walked a hard and stony path that demanded study, reflection and effort. They were people struggling with the nature of good and evil, struggling with the very idea of God and what that had to mean. They were searchers and philosophers, ascetics.

That Alhazred's travels would take him to Damascus, tells us that he is still searching for answers. The existential crisis that sent him wandering and mad into the desert was never truly resolved. Instead, recovered, he continues to search, to struggle, to question. He has become a seeker of esoteric knowledge, an explorer of arcane knowledge, struggling to find a path back to Allah.

One of the favorite metaphors was to describe the comparison between mundane reality and divine reality as the same relationship as between a painting, no matter how skillfully or brilliantly executed, and the real subject of that painting. In short, the imperfect representation or copy, and the real thing.

The metaphor of the Gnostics is remarkable, because they seem to be on the verge of postulating a higher dimensioned reality. A painting is a two dimensional image representing a three dimensional object. The inference here is that our three dimensional reality is only an image or a reflection of a multi-dimensioned greater reality.

Clearly Alhazred is borrowing the Gnostic metaphor, but instead of paintings or visual images, he's using sounds.

Why?

It's his Arabic-Islamic background. The Koran forbids visual representations, even before Mohamed, visual representations had never really been a part of Arabic culture.

The visual metaphor is uncomfortable for him. Indeed, it is literally alien to his culture and upbringing. He casts about for a medium to re-set the metaphor and invents a world of sound and music. And it is an effective metaphor, since it allows him to depict the S'glhuo as genuinely alien, a level of existence whose main quality is its differentness, not its inferiority.

Would Alhazred have believed his own metaphor? Would he really have believed in the beings of the Gulf of S'glhuo?

Almost certainly not. It was a device allowing him to get his head around his real philosophical constructs. Early on, he says little is known of beings of other dimensions, at the end of his passage, he reassures us that they can do little harm. In short, they're mostly unknown and irrelevant to Alhazred... Unreal. Or possibly not, but the key for him is.

But, of course, like any good poet or teller of instructive tales, he needs to polish the story up. After all, the more people believe in the reality, the more they'll take it as a meaningful lesson. He does this in two ways.

One is dragging old Ibn Schacabao out and attributing the story to him. Ibn Schacabao is either a recognized authority who he can attribute the story too and therefore lend it some authenticity.

Or Ibn Schacabao is a literary device that Alhazred pulls out of a hat to avoid having to answer tough questions of how *he* knows these things. Either way, by attributing the story to a real or imaginary third party, we add a veneer of weight and authenticity to the story.

The other device he uses is the 'explanation technique.' All this stuff about S'glhuo being made of sound and the barrier between their world and ours occasionally growing thin... that explains to us why 'when sourceless sounds occur, we may justly look to the denizens of S'glhuo.'

In short, Alhazred makes this tale an explanation for a phenomenon in the natural world. It's another example of all those 'little creation' myths, such as how the bear lost his tail, or why crocodiles always smile.

Nevertheless, it fits in neatly with Alhazred's notions of races preceding or beyond the human sphere, and it is likely that the Necronomicon referred to many such tales and races, which were taken literally by subsequent readers.

It is in Damascus and through Gnosticism that Alhazred makes peace with his broken faith and broken soul. He will never be a true Muslim again. But he learns to live in the world, and to live in the Muslim world, even if it is just a passing shadow.

The Secret of the Sleeping God

But who was Alhazred really?

From **Encyclopedia Britannica**, 1969.

"Kuthayyir ibn 'Abd al-Rahman al-Mulahi, also known as Kuthayyir 'Azza was a poet born to a Yemeni tribe in the Arabian city of Medina in 660 and died 723 C.E. He was born immediately after the First Fitna (first Muslim civil war) 656-661, and was a youth during the Second Fitna (second Muslim war) 683-685 which took place around Medina.

He lived for a time in Egypt, for a time starting probably around 685, where he became a favorite of the governor there, Aziz ibn

An endless impossible unfulfilled love for a woman named Azza. A woman he could never have. A woman he'd spend his life dreaming of. A woman barely aware of him.

Azza, as in Aza-Thoth.

Kuthayyir was a real person, not some creation of some New England pulp writer.

Feel free to look him up.

What do you think his life was like?

Kuthayyir was undoubtedly an intelligent and cultured man; he must have been a devout man, a good Muslim. No one but a good Muslim could have risen so high as to associate so readily with the rich and powerful.

And yet there must have been more to his life. He was a Yemeni in Medina. He was a Shia in a Sunni caliphate. His success came from penning tributes to the famous and the powerful, yet he was not himself one of them.

Instead, he'd lived through the second Fitna (civil war), had seen and observed enough to be acutely aware of the flaws and failings of those he praised so extravagantly. He had an intimate awareness of both the cynicism and hypocrisy of the ruling class, and the cruelties that life had for those below.

The center of his emotional life was an unfulfilled and unfulfillable passion for a woman he could never have by the restrictions of his society.

In many ways, he was a man on the outside of his world, devout, yes, faithful, yes, moving in the highest ranks, but never quite a part of his world, his place. In subtle ways, he was a stranger in the society that he belonged to.

It's tempting to wonder what such a man would have made of Egypt's ancient monuments and storied history. Would he have simply shrugged as less thoughtful men might have, or would he, like the fictional Alhazred, have found the ground slipping away beneath his feet?

It is easy to imagine a man like Kuthayyir following the path we have described for Alhazred. The devout and loyal servant of the Caliphate warning of buried sorcery, the fascination with timeless relics, the doubts and dark nights of the soul and the crushing existential terror.

As a poet, would he not have written of his reflections and anguish? In Arabic society poets had great license, celebrations of romance and drunkenness were tolerated, but this was too far.

The worm that would have gnawed at Kuthayyir, the existential despair, the mad raving, that was blasphemy and apostasy. It would not have been tolerated, and even if it were, it was completely incompatible with the comfortable station and career Kuthayyir had made for himself.

A pseudonym would be necessary, a false name was vital. We said at the beginning that Alhazred was a fictional identity. But the real question is whose fiction? Whose identity?

Cthulhu is the one Alhazred deity who cannot be traced back to its source.

But perhaps the source of Cthulhu is closer to home.

Khuthulu?

Khutayyir?

Is one a corruption of another? Perhaps a transposition of letters and a morphing of 'r' to 'l', perhaps an affectionate pet name or nickname from childhood or forbidden romance.

Who was Cthulhu?

A being trapped beneath the sea, helpless, waiting and dreaming, while blind oblivious Azathoth occupied the center of its universe.

The sea a metaphor for unconsciousness, for isolation. A being trapped and helpless in its existence.

Was Cthulhu, dreaming endlessly in sunken Ry'leh a metaphor for Kuthayyir, trapped in his life, waiting and dreaming, blind Azza, oblivious to his love, insensately occupying the center of his universe.

Was Kuthayyir a man who traveled into the void, into existential despair? Was he a man whose faith eroded away, and left him shivering in a vast emptiness, a speck aware of his insignificance?

Was the only real thing left to him his desperate enduring love for a woman he could never have, in a world that left him trapped?

And did he place his torment at the center of his forbidden writings, a version of himself, a being trapped in an alien world, dead and dreaming, waiting for the stars to change so that he could rise again.

"That is not dead which can eternal lie.
From H.P. Lovecraft's story **'Call of Cthulhu'** 1926

Quote: *And with strange æons even death may die."*

And here the story should end. Kuthayyir lived out his life, writing tributes to the mighty, and poems to an unattainable love, and in the end, he died, as we all do. He probably loved and worshiped, despaired and suffered dark nights of the soul, as this is the human condition. He may have written of his torments and used a pen name, or perhaps he did not.

But the story does not quite end. Kuthayyir poured his existential despair into writing, as a poet is wont to do. He wrote under a pen name, perhaps something like Alhazred, which would have been safer to do.

These works, these poems, these writings, these mad ravings and despairing treatises came down to us through history. Hardly mainstream, but perhaps it might find a life as a work of abstruse philosophy, of speculation, of passion on the furthest fringes of Islamic letters.

In 1885, Sir Richard Francis Burton, an explorer and adventurer, released an English translation of 1001 Arabian Nights in ten volumes. The series, originally sexually explicit, later bowdlerized by a man named Lane, created a sensation in English society. There was suddenly a fascination, a mania for Arabian tales. The east became mysterious, romantic, full of marvels.

It was the Harry Potter series of its day, and like the Harry Potter series it inspired its sequels and imitations in profusion. No less a personality than Edgar Allen Poe wrote a pastiche of Scheherazade's tales.

Publishers, particularly rival publishers, were desperate for new Arabian tales, tales of lost cities, exotic beings and strange wonders. They were hungry for it, eager, hysterical.

Dollar signs danced in front of their eyes as they sought and grasped for more Arabian tales, whether authentically Arabian or written by enterprising con men.

Into this overheated, frenzied environment, Kuthayyir's strange manuscript fell into the hands of an eager publisher, been rendered into English, imaginatively illustrated with fanciful landscapes and creatures, and released to fall quickly by the wayside as usually happens with attempts to ride the tails of a phenomenon.

It wasn't called the Necronomicon, but perhaps it was titled something suggestive. Book of the Dead Arab, or Tale of the Lost City, something like that.

It would have come out to great expectations from its publisher, its strange subject matter would not have captivated, it would have sunk quickly away, forgotten by all and sundry, except for a few orphan copies sitting unremarked in obscure bookstores.

Bookstores are full of orphan books, unloved, abandoned, sitting on shelves in their little corners of oblivion, most of them forgotten and unread. It happens all the time, because this is the way the world is.

Turn now to Howard Philips Lovecraft. Born 1890. He never really knew his father, a man who succumbed to psychosis from tertiary syphilis in 1893 and died in an institution in 1898. But he didn't suffer for lack of love. He was raised by his mother and two doting aunts, and his grandfather, Whipple Van Buren Phillips provided a masculine presence. If his home wasn't the typical environment, it was still as sheltering and nurturing as any young boy might expect.

Young Howard was a child prodigy, reciting poetry by two, writing poems by six, fascinated by science, by chemistry and astronomy; he was a voracious reader almost from the start. His grandfather delighted in and encouraged his reading, providing him with the Odyssey, Bullfinch's Fables. Howard particularly loved the Arabian Nights. It fascinated him; he dreamt of it, he imagined himself in the role of the heroes of the stories. His youthful soul thrilled to it.

And then, somehow, something happened. He had a nervous breakdown at the age of ten. How can a child of ten, a brilliant, precocious child, a child in a secure and loving environment, have a nervous breakdown?

Perhaps his grandfather, Whipple Phillips, browsing some obscure corner of some obscure bookstore found a slim little volume of Arab tales, decided that this was just the thing precocious grandson, so obsessed with all things Arab, and brought it home. Imagine Howard Philips Lovecraft reading it.

Kuthayyir becomes Cthulhu. Perhaps it was the poet himself that did this, burying hmself twice metaphorically, first as the observer, Alhazred and then as the dreamer, Cthulhu. Perhaps it was the publisher, or a sloppy translator or an inexpert typesetter. Perhaps it was Howard who made one into another.

Imagine an innocent, brilliant, ten year old boy following Kuthayyir's footsteps, absorbing his mounting elemental horror without understanding it. Mouthing, sounding out words he's never heard pronounced, Kuthayyir reads as Kuthayli, then Cthulhu.

Imagine this unwary child, exposed to Kuthayyir's abyss, to the awful crushing knowledge that even faith is mortal, that the whole world so safe and secure is merely an island, transient and ephemeral as a soap bubble in a vast an uncaring universe stretching through time and space, a time and space peopled by alien unknowable beings.

Imagine this boy plunged unprepared and unsuspecting into an abyss the likes of which existentialist philosophers like Camus and Sartre had yet to wrestle with.

Imagine Kuthayyir's loneliness, his despair, his madness, the pain of his unattainable love, his madness, the emptiness he saw and felt in every particle of his existence, the cosmic horror he saw surrounding his small world, imagine all of that, come crashing down on a small, innocent, unsuspecting boy in New England, who only half understands it.

Imagine the abyss that slowly opened beneath that boy.

The tragedy was that Howard was brilliant. If he had been less gifted, less perceptive, it might have all gone over his head, and confused, he would have put the book away and gone out to play, as any other boy might, and it would all be forgotten by suppertime.

But the boy, Howard Philips Lovecraft read it and understood it, or understood enough of it. And it destroyed him.

His life could never be the same after that. The abyss opened up, his mind mercifully broke and he had his nervous breakdown.

The book was forgotten, its emptiness and despair was too awful for his innocent mind to remember. But his life was ruined. Gone was the possibility of a normal youth, of adolescent love, of manhood and career, love and marriage and children, all that wiped away. Howard Lovecraft passed his teenage years as a hermit, he found himself unfit for work, terrified by the world, haunted by an abyss he couldn't name.

Instead, inevitably, he found himself compelled to write. Names and images came to him in dreams. Buried passages unfurled from his subconscious as he wrote.

Kuthayyir's abyss haunted him. He wrote dark and obsessive tales of an endless, alien cosmos. He wrote that if we could, even momentarily, truly see the truth of the world, it would destroy us, as it had destroyed him, as it had destroyed the mad Arab before him. He wrote of the abyss, he had no choice, there was nothing else.

Kuthayyir ibn 'Abd al-Rahman al-Mulahi, a mere Medieval Arab poet, without meaning to, without wanting to, had found himself looking into a darkness, an existential void, that consumed him.

Thirteen hundred years later Kuthayyir's abyss would transcend the restrictions of space and time to consume the life of an innocent New England boy in a continent not even imagined, to steal his future and replace it with the twisted contours of its own image.

The End

Acknowledgements

And while I'm here, let's give credit where credit is due.

Regarding Life, Love and the Necronomicon, the quotes are actually genuine. Or authentic. Or something. All of them are actual 'quotes from the Necronomicon' taken principally from Lovecraft's stories, but also from Lovecraft's contemporaries and correspondents, notably E. Hoffman Price, Clark Ashton Smith, and August Derleth, all of whom are safely long dead and their work in public domain. The one exception being a quote from a Ramsay Campbell story, which just seemed so perfectly suited to introduce Gnosticism that I couldn't help it. Campbell is still with us, and a better and more famous writer than I'll ever be, so I hope that he doesn't mind I cribbed a little quote from him.

For the record, these and many other 'Necronomicon' quotes have been assembled and compiled by Dan Clore, copyright 1997-2006. It was an invaluable reference for the story, and while the intention of the quotes was 'ooga booga' many more of them can be reinterpreted, as an existential journey of a man struggling with his faith.

The Black Pharaoh and the Nameless City can be reinterpreted as legends of Akhenaton, for instance. Of course, doing that would have extended this story into a novella length, and that seemed a bit too much. The first draft was twice as long. In the end, I culled my favourite quotes and regretfully discarded others.

I'm quite proud of my unique little reconstructions of the Lovecraft mythos.

What else? The stuff about 'off switches' for genes, in the Sasquatch Kid story is true enough, or at least consistent with recent theory.

Fossils was originally published in Daikaiju, a best-selling Australian anthology by Robert Hood and Robin Pen, and Tell Me published in After Hours magazine published out of L.A, by William G. Raley. I want to thank both of these publications for giving me hope and sustenance.

Most of these stories were written and reviewed by my old writers group, which included Steve Erikson, David Keck, Ian Ross, Mireille Theriault, Scott Ellis and Sean Garrity, and of course, were reviewed by my then wife, Anna Maria (Boudreau)Valdron. The stories wouldn't be what they were without them, so I'm spreading the blame around.

I want to give a shout out a shout out to Eldon Ardiente, my cover artist, who did a wonderful job. Check out his work at http://www.eldenardiente.daportfolio.com/. He takes commissions.

Thank you All

Note, More Books by the Author

Hello! If you've skipped to the end, looking for an apology, well... Sorry? Also, no refunds.

Thank you for taking the time out to read or listen to my little book. If you've made it all the way here, then I'm just going to assume you liked it.

Let me tell you about my other books.

And while you're here, let me ask a favour. If you liked this, say nice things in a review. If that's too much, just toss me a couple of stars. Writing is a solitary, lonely pursuit and actually getting some feedback or appreciation is a wonderful thing.

But there's more to it. It's about trying to get out there. There are a lot of people writing a lot of books, and it can get hard to get noticed. Reviews help.

And speaking of writing more....'

Check out my Website, at denvaldron.com

HEARTS IN DARKNESS
A Trilogy of Horror Collections

Three Collections of Subversive Horror and Dark Fantasy.

Giant Monsters Sing Sad Songs – The connection between the author of the Necronomicon and a boy in Providence; a girl who meets the last sasquatch, a poet who shares abandoned Tokyo with a Kaiju, and more…

What Devours Also Hungers – The unkillable killers in masks are recruited into the army, vampires and their hunters, clever serial killers, monsters, ghosts and more….

There Are No Doors in Dark Places…..

FUNNY FANTASY
And COMIC SCIENCE FICTION

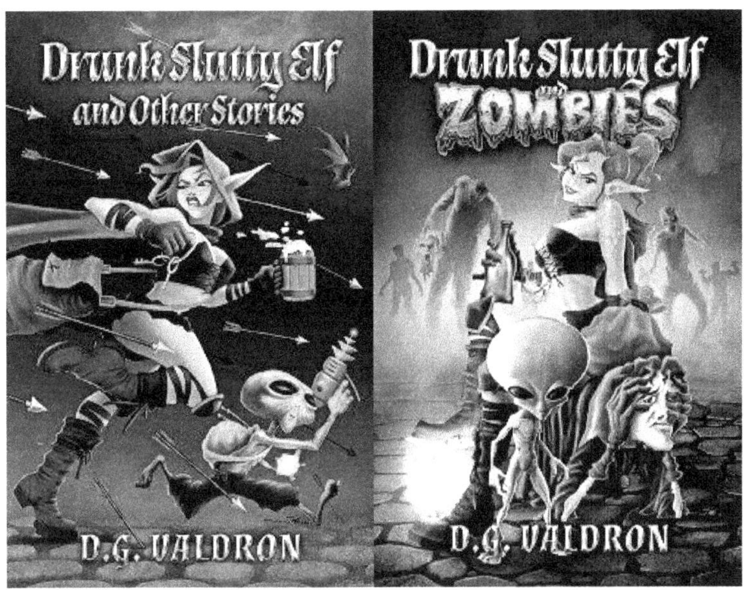

DRUNK SLUTTY ELF AND OTHER STORIES
Plus
DRUNK SLUTTY ELF AND ZOMBIES

Two volumes of savage, satirical, subversive wicked, funny, frantic science fiction and fantasy. Demented ghost hunters, frustrated aliens, horny giants, drunken elves, sneaky ghosts, wayward barbarians and many more.

A Dark Fantasy of Murder and Redemption

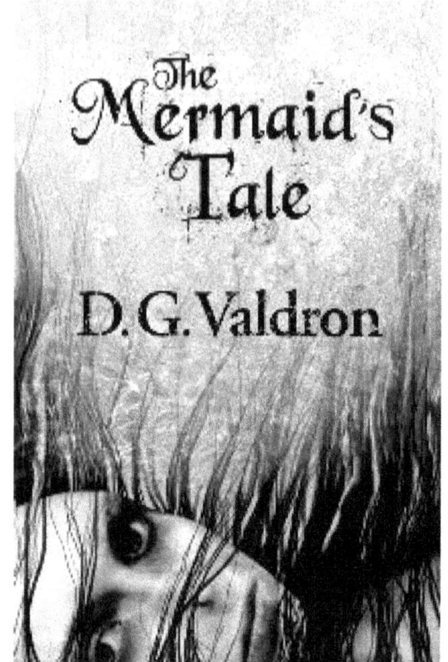

There's a City where all the races come together uneasily, descending into civil war.

There's a Mermaid, murdered cruelly her people distraught and crying out for justice.

There's an Orc, the lowest and the worst, her mission: Solve the murder, before it all comes crashing down.

And there's something else... this world's first serial killer.

Available only as an Audiobook

ALTERNATE REALITIES
A Trilogy or Strange New Worlds
The Other books

The Dawn of Cthulhu - The Secret History of H.P. Lovecraft's Cthulhu Cult; Lost Continents Found – real and legendary; The Monsters of Sesame Street, is a light hearted examination of Muppets as if they were actual animals.

The Fall of Atlantis – Retroverse, An Accidental Cinematic Universe of 50's Sci Fi movies, Greenland Without the Ice, Rome Crosses the Altantic, and the Rise and Fall of Atlantis, an ecological catastrophe.

The Bear Cavalry, the True (Not!) History of the Icelandic Bears, an off the wall, short novel about the Viking domestication of bears, their evolution into a medieval cavalry Bonus novelette, The Sharebear Apocalypse.

AXIS OF ANDES
NEW WORLD WAR
A History of WWII in South America

Berlin, 1937, Adolph Hitler and his cabinet meet with a strange delegation from Ecuador. The delegates from the small South American nation beg for help, fearing an impending invasion from their rival, Peru. What happens at that meeting sets in motion a chain of events that sets the entire continent on fire. By the time it's done, millions are dead, nations are in ruins, and the map of Latin America will be changed beyond recognition.

THE PIRATE HISTORIES OF DOCTOR WHO

The greatest, Doctor Who fan films ever made, the history of animated Doctor Who, audio Doctor Who, the Stage Plays, explorations of the peculiarities of copyright, the developments of new technologies, the evolution of fan culture, and behind the scenes skullduggery. These books are full of new and entertaining insights and revelations that you'll love.

LEXX Unauthorized, the Series

LEXX Unauthorized about the making of a show about a giant space bug that blows up planets, the cowardly security guard who is its captain, and the undead assassin, runaway love slave, and robot head who form its crew.

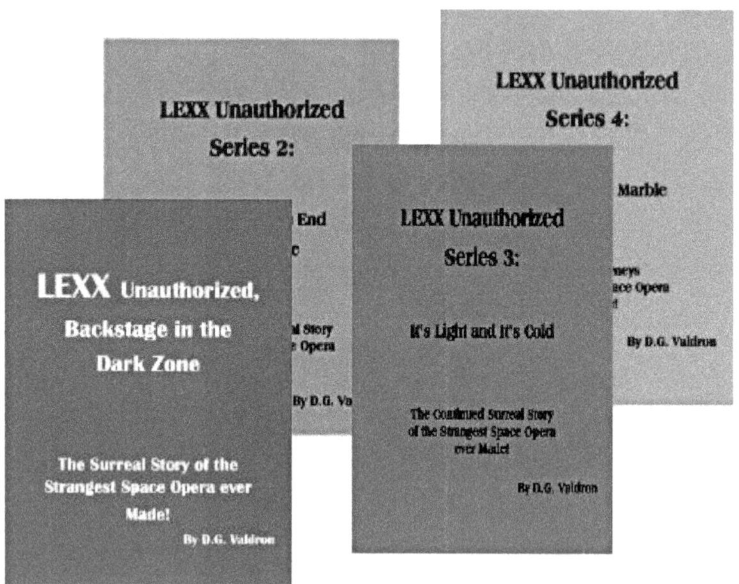

Originally billed as '*Star Trek's Evil Twin*,' the cultiest of cult sci fi, LEXX's forte was black humor, startling visuals, big ideas, and a sensibility that had more to do with surrealists like Jodorowsky or Bunuel than mainstream science fiction. And, as unconventional as it was onscreen, the story of how it came to be is even more bizarre.

STARLOST UNAUTHORIZED
And the Quest for Canadian Identity

The series that was Harlan Ellison's nemesis. The most
controversial series in the history of sci fi television. This
exhaustively researched book, based on interviews with some
of the stars and writers, brings a fresh new interpretation of
of the Starlost, and a re-evaluation of the series and its themes
in the context of the 1970s crisis of Canadian nationalism.

TWILIGHT OF ECHELON
Published by
AT BAY PRESS

Based on the work of famed artist Robert Pasternak the book features paintings from Pasternak's Echelon series, accompanied by stories written independently by D.G. Valdron, Lovern Kindzierski, Alex Passey and Blaise Moritz.

www.ingramcontent.com/pod-product-compliance
Lightning Source LLC
Chambersburg PA
CBHW070722010826

48977CB00006B/397